DEMON MAGIC

Book 3

The Mage's Daughter Trilogy

S.A. BECK

This is a work of fiction. Names, characters, organizations,places, events, and incidents are either products of the author's imagination or are used fictitiously.

DEMON MAGIC: THE MAGE'S DAUGHTER TRILOGY
Copyright © 2017 by S.A. BECK. All rights reserved.

ISBN: 978-1-987859-41-6

CONTENTS

CHAPTER 1
Road Trip through a Broken Nation

On an ordinary day, the scenery passing by outside the window of the car might have excited Ines Salgado. Growing up in London, she had never spent much time in the countryside. Even when her parents took her and her brother, Toby, on holidays, it was usually to another city somewhere in Europe or a beach where they could all relax with sand between their toes. She had never seen the beauty rural England had to offer, especially up here in the craggy hills and isolated villages of North Yorkshire. Trees, hedgerows, drystone walls, and centuries-old farmhouses were scattered across a rolling patchwork of fields, many of them filled with soft, docile flocks of sheep, their woolly coats making them look like clouds that had fallen out of the sky and into the hands of farmers.

But it was hard, on a day like this one, for Ines to let go of the stress and appreciate the beauty around her. She knew what had really fallen from the heavens, and it wasn't a scatter of soothing wool. It was angels and demons, falling through the gaps in the fractured Barrier of Mercy, the magical wall that had always held the worlds apart. Those denizens of Heaven and Hell brought wild emotions and the chaos that followed them. In the past few weeks, Ines had fought the monstrous forces of both sides. She had fended off angels, demons, and mages of the human ministry that tried to deal with them, and whose secrecy had left the world unprepared. She had hurt people, even killed the creatures that came against her, and she in turn had come close to death. But even after all of that, she knew that there was worse to come.

"Could we please have some music?" Ines asked. "I don't mind what it is. I just need a distraction. If I spend much longer chasing my own thoughts, then I'll go mad."

"No," replied Tamsin Shaw, who was driving. Her short blond hair bounced against the side of her face, and she blew a strand out of her eyes. "If there's any chance we can hear trouble coming, then we need to take it."

"Because we can hear so much over the noise of the engine." Damon's voice was so thick with sarcasm that Ines could almost hear him rolling his eyes. She didn't need to glance at the backseat to picture his wry expression.

"When you kids are old enough to drive yourselves, then you can control the stereo," Shaw said.

"I'm seventeen," Damon said. "I could have my license by now."

"Do you?"

"No."

"Well, then."

Shaw yanked hard on the wheel as they headed into a tight bend. The car tilted, and Ines felt her stomach churn. It flipped again as they came out of the bend and shot over a hump in the road. Shaw wasn't slowing down for safety, never mind the speed limit, but she never faltered. Apparently, her Ministry of Occult Affairs training had included a section on race-car driving.

"I am older than any of you," Rumiel said from the seat behind Shaw. "Older than this device or even your nation."

"You look like a teenager," Shaw said. "You act like a teenager. Angel or not, I'm going to keep treating you like a teenager."

They drove on, the only sound the engine and the occasional thunk as they drove over a pothole. They had agreed to take a back route up to Durham in an effort to avoid trouble. This was less about angels and demons and more about the Ministry, whose servants had been hunting them on Elizabeth Oldfield's orders.

That and the other conflicts consuming Britain.

They reached a junction, and Shaw turned left, taking them onto a larger road. It was deserted, with no traffic heading in either direction.

"I need a rest," she said. "And we need fuel."

A few miles on, they reached a petrol station. The shutters were closed despite the fact that it was only the middle of the afternoon. Shaw slowed the car and kept one hand off the wheel, ready to summon magic, as she drove onto the forecourt.

"Damon, you're with me," Shaw said as she stopped the car and stepped out. "Ines, Rumiel, fuel up and guard the car."

"I do not know how to 'fuel up,'" Rumiel said, stretching his athletic body as he too opened his door and got out.

"Of course you don't," Damon said as he hurried after Shaw, a gangling figure in black following the confident woman in her battered grey suit.

"I can do it." Ines got out and went to the pump, keeping her eyes fixed on the task at hand. She had seen Rumiel smiling and trying to catch her eye as she emerged, and she didn't want to deal with what was between them. But as she grabbed the fuel nozzle and started filling the tank, Rumiel stepped around to face her, his face filled with an idiotic grin.

"Ines Salgado." He reached out a hand, brushing her cheek with the tips of his fingers. Despite herself, she shivered at the touch. He was so beautiful, the immortal young man with his blond hair, his muscled body, and his warm, soft skin. "I am glad that we travel together on this quest."

"Listen, Rumiel," she said, finally looking him in the eye. "When we kissed on the train... I'm not sure that's going to happen again."

"Why are you uncertain?" Rumiel asked, his face falling. "Was it not a good kiss?"

"It was a great kiss," Ines admitted. "But things are complicated. There's so much going on. You were fighting against us in Manchester. I need time to get past that, and to think about what I want."

Time to decide whether she wanted him or Damon, she admitted in the confines of her mind. But Rumiel didn't need to know that. Ideally, neither he nor Damon would ever find out. She needed both the angel and her half-demon best friend on her side right now, and the thought of upsetting either wasn't one she could face.

"I understand." Rumiel withdrew his hand. "I do not have a mother, but if I did, then her captivity would distress me. But fear not— we will rescue her, just as surely as we will repair the Barrier of Mercy."

"I wish I had your confidence," Ines said, returning the fuel nozzle to its station and screwing the cap back into place.

"Do you believe in me?" Rumiel asked.

"You turned against your kind to protect me," Ines said. "You fought Michael and the Flaming Host. How could I not believe in you?"

"Then believe that I can achieve anything if it will make you happy," Rumiel said. "And so we will win."

Absurd as it was, his boldness made her smile, and some of the tension eased from her body.

"Hold it right there," a voice commanded.

Ines turned to see half a dozen camouflaged soldiers emerging from behind a hedgerow. Their assault rifles were aimed at her and Rumiel. The sight put a new weight of dread in her stomach.

"Raise your hands," the lead soldier said, "and tell me which side you're on."

"Side of what?" Ines said, raising her hands. Rumiel followed suit.

"Parliamentary or patriot," one of the other soldiers said, glaring at her.

"We're not with any side," Ines said. "We're just driving through."

"Nobody just drives through a warzone," the lead soldier said. He and his men walked slowly towards them, guns still raised, those at the end of the line turning to survey their surroundings. "Which means you're agents, and probably hostile ones. Turn around and put your hands on the car."

Ines tried to suppress her fear and not to glance towards the door of the petrol station. Even if the two of them were captured, as long as the others were still at large, their mission could continue.

"It is not for you to order me around," Rumiel said, an angry edge entering his voice. "I am Rumiel of the Golden Flight."

"What the hell's the Golden Flight?" one of the soldiers asked. "Some new unit Parliament's set up?"

"I am nothing to do with Hell," Rumiel exclaimed. His hands came down as he took a step away from the car, out into the open. "I will not—"

"Hands up again, or I shoot," the lead soldier yelled.

Then everything seemed to happen at once. Golden wings burst from Rumiel's back, and he lit up with a light that made even the concrete beneath their feet golden. There was an electronic *bing* as the door of the petrol station opened, revealing Damon and Shaw. Half the soldiers turned to face them, and all opened fire.

Ines flung herself to the ground. Throwing out her arm, she landed in a breakfall and rolled behind the car, the only cover within twenty feet. As the bark of the guns announced a hail of bullets filling the air, she glanced around in fear for her friends.

At the other end of the car, Rumiel had produced a flaming sword from thin air and was spinning it in front of him, creating a blur of magical flame that melted the bullets as they hit, molten metal spattering the ground. In the doorway, Shaw grimaced as she flung up a magical barrier four times the size of the shields Ines had seen her produce before. She trembled at the strain of pouring so much magic not into her natural gifts, but into the forms the Ministry taught its people. Bullets ricocheted off the glowing barrier, striking the ground and sending chips of concrete flying.

The soldiers swore in amazement but kept firing. A bullet penetrated the shutters and shattered the window beyond. Glass flew, and blood ran from Shaw's shoulder.

Damon raised his hand, the gleaming disk of his pocket watch held out before him. His eyes went black as he chanted and then stepped out from behind Shaw's shield.

The two soldiers nearest Damon yelped in surprise, dropped their guns, and backed away, staring down at their hands. Their fingernails were growing so fast that Ines could see it happen. Blood ran from one man's palm as the nails jutted mercilessly into his skin. Hair streamed from beneath their helmets, streaks of grey appearing as it ran down their backs.

"Pull back!" the lead soldier yelled. "Pull back now!"

Three of the soldiers backed away slowly, still pointing their guns uncertainly at the travelers. The others turned tail and ran, one of the men Damon had affected whimpering in terror at the way his body had betrayed him.

Letting down her shield, Shaw leaned against the doorframe. Her hair fell away from her face, revealing the scars a magical attack in Manchester had left on her right cheek.

"There's likely to be more of that," she said. "We found a radio playing in there. News reports say it's now full-on civil war. Something similar is happening in Europe, and there are reports of bombing raids between Russia and China. I'd say that the world really is going to Hell, but we all know that the problem is Hell coming here."

"Are you all right?" Ines stood and walked over to the exhausted-looking mage.

"I'm just relieved that none of those bullets hit a fuel tank." Shaw gestured behind her into the petrol-station shop. "There's nobody manning the till, but there is plenty of food. I suggest we grab refreshments and move on before those soldiers return with reinforcements."

As they walked into the shop, Damon brushed his fingers against Ines's and made to take her hand. She snatched it away and thrust her hands into the pocket of her hoodie.

Her fingers closed around the object her father had placed in there before she'd left him and Toby behind. A small patch of denim with a protective ward embroidered onto it in thread so thick that she could make out the pattern with her fingertips. Glancing back at the bullet-riddled concrete and the intact car, she wondered if the ward had already kept her safe, or if she was just lucky.

Whether it came down to luck or to magic, she hoped it worked again, because one thing was certain—there were far worse threats ahead.

CHAPTER 2
Demons and Angels

"Two more hours, and we should be in Durham." Shaw traced a line along the map spread out on the car's hood.

"That long?" Ines asked, her voice little more than a groan. She was sick of being on the road. Sick of leg cramps from sitting in the same position for hours. Sick of the way the seat belt dug into her neck any time she dozed off and her head started to tip over. Sick of the awkwardness she felt stuck in the car with Damon and Rumiel.

Spending time with either of them alone would have been fantastic, but being around them both was a nightmare. She could feel the big stupid smile that spread across her face when Rumiel looked at her the right way, or when Damon said something funny or thoughtful. That smile made her glance nervously at the other one, afraid he would work out that something was up. Even moments of pleasure now made her squirm.

"That long," Shaw said. She folded away the map and leaned against the hood, stretching her slender legs out in front of her. "We could have been there in a quarter of the time if we'd driven directly. But then we would have been running into roadblocks and military convoys, flights of angels raising people's spirits, and throngs of demons feeding off their hate. This way, we avoid the worst of all those things."

"I don't think we've entirely avoided them," Damon said, staring across the road.

They had stopped on the shoulder of a quiet back road running along a hillside, a place obscure enough to not have road markings. It could just about have coped with traffic going both ways as long as there was nothing wider than a mini. On the side where the hill sloped up above them were a selection of rocks large enough to use as seats while they ate more of the food they'd taken from the petrol station—Rumiel gobbling chocolate and jelly sweets with childish glee, Ines nibbling on crisps, Damon drinking a cup of coffee that had gone cold an hour ago.

Suddenly, her friend tensed.

On the other side of the road, a figure was approaching across the fields. He looked at first like a man, albeit an old-fashioned one, in his loose-hanging black suit and broad-brimmed hat. As he came closer, Ines caught a glimpse of the features hiding in the shadow of that hat, and she understood what had set Damon on edge. A pale mask of fake skin drooped from a visage with a hooked nose, jagged black teeth, and bulbous green eyes. It lurched from one leg to the other, moving swiftly and yet as though the process of walking were completely alien to it.

"Should we go?" Ines asked, placing a hand on the knife she kept hidden in a sheath up her other sleeve.

"No," Damon said, setting aside the coffee as he stood up. "I'm going to have to have this conversation sooner or later—might as well do it now."

Both Shaw and Rumiel stiffened as they realized what was approaching. Shaw kept her face neutral but held her hands loosely by her sides, ready for action. Rumiel glared in open hostility. Both had dedicated their lives to battling demons and their influence. Now one was coming towards them, and for once, violence was not a solution.

The creature reached the opposite side of the road and stopped. Sweeping its hat from its head, it curled forward in a low bow, while strings of writhing grey hair hung from its head.

"Viscount Demi-Chron," the creature said. "I bring greetings from your father and from all attending upon the court of Lord Chron. He is proud of your progress, and we all wait eagerly for the next actions of the heir to our master's throne."

"Straighten up, Eldervain," Damon said. "Life is enough of a mockery without you playing the posing courtier in the middle of nowhere."

"There is no posing to this," Eldervain said, returning his hat to his head. "It is very much a matter of substance. You have taken on great power, son of Chron, and we all wish to see what you will do with it."

"Nothing that need concern you—that's what I'm doing," Damon said.

"I must beg to differ, oh inheritor of greatness. Yours is a power that places you among the upper echelons of demonkind. You are all but a lord in your own right now. Your actions are the concern of many, among them those who await you at court."

"I have business in the world. And even if I didn't, I would have no desire to visit Hell."

"Then perhaps its denizens could visit you?" Eldervain stepped forwards, hands outstretched. "Many are eager to call upon you, to seek your patronage and discover what they might do to earn your favor."

"If they want to be in my good books, then they should just stay away," Damon said, drawing a watch from his pocket. "And you should do the same, Eldervain. Whatever my heritage, I'm still human, and that's the life I choose. I'll defend it by force if I have to."

"Threats and posturing." Eldervain grinned, revealing row after row of filthy pointed teeth. "Your father will be proud."

He bowed once more and walked away across the field.

Damon was shaking as he sat back down on the rock next to Ines. She placed a reassuring hand on his shoulder, and he leaned his head against it, taking deep, calming breaths.

"It's okay," Ines said. "If you don't want to deal with them, you don't have to."

"Really?" Damon looked her in the eyes. "Because if they decide to come for me, I'm not sure I can fight them off."

"Maybe Ines can." Shaw stood where Eldervain had been, sipping from a can of Coke and watching the demon as he shambled into the distance. "The girl who can fight angels and demons without magic, someone unheard of in all my studies and years in the Ministry. If anyone can chase away your would-be minions, it's her."

"And if Ines commands it, then I will assist," Rumiel said, grinning. "It will be no burden to cut down the forces of Hell."

"Great," Damon said. "More fighting."

* * *

The demons weren't the only ones looking for them.

Half an hour later, as Shaw wove the car through the remains of a burned-out military convoy, Ines looked up and saw a bright figure hanging in the sky above them. Another joined it, and as the two descended in slow circles, she saw for certain what she had feared from the start—they were angels, and they were on the hunt.

"Rumiel, there are some of yours out there," she said, pointing at them. "Do you think they can tell we're here?"

"I do not know," Rumiel replied. "It depends upon who they are. Sanctus has little gift for anything beyond the brawl. Hernais, on the other hand, can track the passage of a soul through the world once he has its scent."

"Great." Ines reached down the side of her seat, picking up one of the assault rifles left behind by the fleeing soldiers. "How easily can any of them fend off bullets?"

"Too easily."

There was a click as Rumiel unfastened his seat belt, and then the whir of his window being wound down.

"I will see if they are of the Blazing Host," he said. "If Michael sent them, then it is best that we know it."

Before anyone could object, he burst out of the car with a thudding of wings through the air, racing towards the shining figures.

"Great." Shaw slammed on the brakes and leaned forward to better see what was happening. Ines stuck her head out of her window, fingers tight around the gun as she watched to see what would happen.

For a moment, it appeared that they had gotten lucky. As Rumiel approached the other angels, all three stopped and hung in the air a hundred feet above the ground, wings flapping as they conversed. Ines began to relax.

Then there was a roar, and fire blasted from the hands of one of the figures, surrounding Rumiel in a ball of flames. Seconds later, he shot out of the inferno, sword swinging. There was a flash, and the other angel went flying backwards, arcing towards the ground.

Rumiel turned to face his other opponent. Too slow bringing his sword around, he did not get the blade up before the angel slammed into him, shoulder to belly. Rumiel's sword vanished, and the two of them grappled in the blue sky, grabbing at wings, punching at faces, trying to get a lock on each other's bodies. Tangled together in their melee, they tumbled from the heavens, heading towards a hill farther down the road.

The car jolted as Shaw hit the accelerator. Ines was flung back in her seat, gun still in hand, as they raced for the area where the figures would land.

The whole world seemed to tremble as the two angels hit the ground, dirt flying as if an artillery shell had just hit. The car screeched around a bend, shot across a junction, and ploughed through a wooden gate into a field, splintered planks hurtling in every direction. Shaw wrenched the steering wheel around, and they skidded to a halt a hundred yards from a crater in the middle of a field of flattened corn.

Ines leapt out and raced towards the crater, from which sounds of violence were emerging along with flashes of light. At the edge, she paused, gun ready, staring down.

The two angels were in the center of the crater, fighting with supernatural power and passion. With a swift movement, Rumiel raised his opponent above his head and slammed him into the ground, dirt flying. A moment later, he was on his back as his opponent swept his legs out from beneath him. The two of them rolled over and over, battering at each other with hands and feet, light bursting in great arcs from their fists. So much magic had flooded into the world, it seemed, that clashes between angels drew power from the very air.

The other angel gained the upper hand, straddling Rumiel, pinning his arms in place. A flurry of blows smashed against Rumiel's face, the light flickering so fast it could have triggered an epileptic fit.

The gun felt useless in Ines's hands. What if Rumiel moved as she fired and she hit him? Or what if she was such a terrible shot that she just hit him anyway? After all, she had never fired a weapon like this before. But she couldn't just stand here, not when Rumiel was in danger.

Swinging the rifle around, she charged down into the crater, letting out a roar of rage. The angel turned as she reached it, and she slammed the butt of the rifle into the side of its perfect white face. A ripple seemed to cross its features as it was flung back, off Rumiel and down in the dirt.

Casting aside the rifle, Ines leapt upon her opponent. He raised his hands, and a glowing knife started to appear in one of them, but Ines was faster. Her blade, a kitchen knife she had kept sharp since her first encounter with a demon, was already in her hand. She slashed across the angel's arm, knife cutting through glowing flesh, and the angelic blade disappeared. As she plunged the knife down towards his chest, the angel heaved them both up out of the dirt, flinging her aside even as she buried the blade in his shoulder. Teeth bared, he pulled the kitchen knife out and cast it aside. He spread his wings wide and flew back up into the sky.

There was a bark of gunfire. The angel jerked, and one of his wings hung limply, but he kept on flying. At the edge of the crater, Shaw stood with the other assault rifle in her hands, smoke drifting from the barrel.

"Better than nothing," she said, lowering the gun.

Rumiel smiled as Ines helped him up, and as he leaned on her, she felt her heart race.

"I knew I could count on you," he said and hugged her tight.

CHAPTER 3
Bellowing God's Name

Night was falling as they parked in a quiet street full of red-brick townhomes. A viaduct loomed above the neighborhood, vast blocks of yellow-grey stone holding train tracks dozen of meters up them. As they got out of the car, a goods train rumbled slowly by on those tracks. Ines could have sworn she felt the shaking through her feet.

"I expected something a bit more impressive," Damon said, looking up and down the street. "If this is one of the holiest cities in England, then I don't think Hell faces much of a challenge."

"You'll see the impressive parts soon enough," Shaw said.

Leaving bags and guns locked in the trunk of the car, the four travelers made their way into town, the teenagers and the angel following Shaw's lead. They crossed a main road near a roundabout, seeing just enough traffic to show that civilization hadn't entirely died. The next street was almost deserted by cars but contained more people than Ines had seen out in the open since they'd left Manchester. Most were making their way between the pubs, bars, and takeout places that filled half the buildings. A few stood around in small groups, smoking, talking, and watching the world go by. None of them seemed particularly interested in the travelers.

"Do they even know there's a war on?" Ines whispered.

"Life carries on," Shaw said. "We're far enough from the front lines for people to feel safe."

With the Barrier of Mercy down, safety was relative. Blurry shapes of angels and demons hovered, largely unseen, at the edges of groups of people. Any time emotion flared, whether excited laughter or angry shouting, some of the creatures nearby grew more substantial. There were not as many as there had been when chaos broke out in London, but then there were not as many people here.

"This place used to be the social heart of the city," Shaw said. "At least for locals. Students tend to stick with their bars and the pubs in the center. But this..." A wave of her hand took in the slightly run-down fronts of bars and shops. "Well, things change."

"This doesn't seem like city-sized nightlife," Damon said. "More inbred market town."

"Durham doesn't count as a city because it's big," Shaw said. "It counts because of this."

They had crossed from the end of the street onto a broad area paved with flagstones that merged into an old but well-kept stone bridge. Emerging from the surrounding shops and bars, they gained a clear view of what lay on the other side of the river.

It took Ines's breath away.

The far bank was a steep slope. Ahead of them, it turned into more shops and houses, with a street that veered off to the left. To the right, trees were just visible in the darkness, swaying in a gentle breeze as they crept down to the river, its surface glittering in the light of the rising moon. But it was what rose up from beyond the trees that was truly stunning.

Straight ahead was a castle. Broad and square, it loomed over the town like a proud but overbearing father. Orange floodlights illuminated its walls so that it shone with a warm glow whose welcome was at odds with its intimidating stone walls and crenellated battlements. It was like something out of a storybook, a fortress overlooking all around with forceful intent.

Yet what lay to the right was even more breathtaking. Cast into the stark white of a vivid ghost by the lights shining up at it, Durham Cathedral towered over even the castle. Its walls were dotted with arches, windows, buttresses, and carvings, giving its pale presence a baroque intricacy. Yet there was nothing delicate about this building. There were no narrow spires, no carefully balanced statues, nothing thin or fragile. Instead, towers as solid as the castle rose towards the heavens, the central one looming over others at each corner of the building. It did not try to coax people in to embrace God through open doors and a welcoming facade. Instead, it asserted his presence over the world around it.

Now Ines understood why this was a holy place.

"My old tutor used to say that most cathedrals sing God's name into our ears," Shaw said in a soft voice, "but Durham bellows it straight into our faces."

"You studied here?" Ines asked.

"It's a good place to go if you want to be a vicar," Shaw said. She frowned as if she had just let go of something precious to her. "I didn't always want to work in the political sort of ministry."

"Is that where the government people are based?" Ines asked, staring in wonder at the cathedral.

"Too divine." Shaw shook her head. "They're up on the hill, hidden away in the university science site. You can explain away a lot if you work next to experimental physicists.

"But the cathedral is still important to the Ministry. It's why they started working here, why it's the biggest Ministry base outside London, and why it's the perfect place both for us to fix the Barrier and for Oldfield to keep feeding off its energies. Not many places have such a rich aura of religious awe."

"So the Ministry will be holding my mother at this science site?"

"It's certainly the place to start. But we'll need to be careful. As my grandfather used to say, if you're going to have to wrestle a bear, at least size him up first."

* * *

"This is ridiculous," Ines snapped. "We should be scouting out the Ministry, not lurking outside someone's house."

"We do have the look of stalkers right now," Damon said. "Is it too harsh to hope the police are busy breaking up fights?"

Shaw glanced up and down the road one more time. Ines followed her gaze, peering into the shadows between lampposts, looking for the twitching of curtains in windows.

"I think we're clear," Shaw said. "If the place were being watched, then the Ministry would have moved on us by now."

With that, she strode out of the alley mouth and across the street. Ines, Damon and Rumiel hurried after her, finding themselves on the doorstep of one of the nondescript terrace houses.

A movement made Ines turn in alarm, drawing her knife as she stared up the street. Heart racing, she stared into the stillness, only to see a mouse staring back at her from next to a garbage bin. Its whiskers twitched, and then it ran away, disappearing into a pile of uncollected trash.

A few bars of jolly doorbell music sounded as Shaw pressed the button. Then there was the shuffling of feet, a pause, and a muffled "Oh my!"

The door swung open, spilling light across them. A large man in a tartan dressing gown and fluffy slippers stood smiling from behind a bushy brown beard.

"Tamsin!" he said. "And you've brought friends. Quick, come in."

He stepped aside, ushering them into his home. As Ines paused in a hallway decorated with dozens of small framed sketches of scenery, the man peered up and down the street then shut the door firmly behind them.

"I hear that you're on the run," he said as he led them into his living room. "How thrilling."

"Timothy Marklew," Shaw said, nodding towards the man, "this is Ines Salgado, Damon Lorus, and Rumiel."

"Doesn't this dashing young man have a surname?" Marklew said as he lingered over shaking Rumiel's hand.

"He's one of the Host," Shaw said.

Marklew frowned.

"Under current circumstances, bringing him here seems a little distasteful," he said. "Some might say hazardous to my health."

"You think that's bad?" Shaw sank into a padded leather armchair. "Damon is the half-demon spawn of Lord Chron."

"Who are you calling spawn?" Damon demanded.

"You're just jealous she thought of it first," Ines said, carefully maneuvering so that she could take the other armchair rather than end up sitting on the sofa next to the boys. If either of them tried to hold her hand or place an arm around her... Well, that was something to deal with later.

"Explanations are clearly in order," Marklew said. "But first, refreshments."

He disappeared down the hallway, reappearing two minutes later with a tray laden with pork pies, pastries, glasses, a bottle of lemonade, another holding port, and one of whiskey. He placed it on a coffee table beneath the large TV. The spread was like the slap-up meal at the end of an Enid Blyton novel, except with more alcohol.

"These three are too young to be drinking," Shaw said.

"Tish posh," Marklew said. "Everybody starts underage."

Despite his words, he only poured port for himself and Shaw, providing the others with lemonade. Then he sat back and listened as Shaw explained what was going on. By the time she finished, he was onto his second glass of the ruby-color-ed liquid, and the hungry travelers had demolished most of the food.

"That makes a lot of things clearer," Marklew said. "There have been some upheavals today at the Ministry, both here and in London. Mixed reports from the other branches too. The place has fractured. Everyone's tense. Reading between the lines of messages from Liverpool, I think the staff there have been fighting, and it hasn't been pretty."

"So Oldfield has lost her support?" Ines asked, leaning eagerly forwards.

"Far from it," Marklew said. "Some people are turning against her, that's for certain, and at least one director has been sounded by the government as a potential replacement."

"Which government?" Damon asked, flipping his pocket watch back and forth in his hands. "I hear we have a few now."

"The parliamentary one," Marklew said. "They still hold London, where most of the bigwigs are."

"If people are turning against her, why do you say she hasn't lost her support?" Ines asked.

Marklew picked up two fresh glasses, poured a finger of whiskey into each, and passed one to Shaw. Closing his eyes, he paused for a moment with his nose over the glass, smiling as he inhaled the smell.

Then he opened his eyes and looked at Ines.

"Salgado?" he asked. "So you're Julie and David's daughter?"

"Oldfield," Ines snapped, her patience wearing thin. "Support. Tell me."

"Someone takes after her mother." Marklew sipped his whiskey and exchanged a wry look with Shaw. "Oldfield still has the most support because she's been a fixture of the Ministry for a long time, and a powerful one. Lots of people owe her favors. Some owe her their entire careers. Many believe in the things she does. Resistance has revitalized their support, animated them as they leap to her aid, sure they will receive favors in return. The Ministry is divided, but she leads the largest part, and by far the most influential."

"They're fighting everyone," Ines said. "Angels, demons, each other—doesn't that count for something?"

"If all those forces could work together, maybe," Marklew said. "But I don't see that happening, do you?"

CHAPTER 4
On Palace Green

Ines woke up in a strange room. Light seeped in around a pair of green velvet curtains, illuminating yellow walls and a bedspread decorated with bold, stylized daisies. She stretched, yawned, scrunched her eyes, and for a moment, enjoyed the feeling of being well rested.

Then she remembered why she was in a strange room, in the house of a man she had only met the night before.

Slipping out from beneath the duvet, she grabbed the sweatpants and T-shirt she had abandoned on the floor and pulled them on. Socks and sneakers followed, neither smelling pleasant. Her hoodie with the cartoon mouse hung over the back of a chair, and she grabbed it before opening the door.

Stepping out onto the landing, she almost tripped over her bag, the one she had left in the car. She flung it onto the bed, closed the door behind her, and headed downstairs towards the smells of coffee and bacon.

Her mouth watered as she reached the kitchen. Mounds of bacon, fried eggs, and toast were piled up on a breakfast bar made of reclaimed railway sleepers. Marklew stood in front of an old iron stove, frying sausages and scrambling more eggs, still dressed in the tartan dressing gown and furry slippers he had worn the night before. Shaw, wearing a pair of men's jeans held up with a belt, and a T-shirt too loose for her but too tight for Marklew, sat on a stool drinking coffee, a laptop open in front of her.

"Help yourself," Marklew said, gesturing towards the food.

Ines poured herself a glass of juice, downed it in a single gulp, and refilled it. Then she started buttering toast.

"Where did you get the clothes?" she asked, looking at Shaw and hoping that, wherever they'd come from, there might also be something fresh in her size. All they'd managed to pick up on the way north had been food and those two rifles. She hadn't worn anything genuinely clean for days.

"They belong to my ex," Marklew said. "Been holding onto them, hoping he would come back. But I fear it's a little late for that now."

Attacking the eggs, bacon, and sausages, Ines felt her energy levels rising. It was great to eat anything that was still fresh and hadn't come out of a plastic package.

"How do we start finding Mum?" she asked.

"We don't yet," Shaw replied, watching her carefully.

A flicker of annoyance ran through Ines. But now that she was better rested, she could accept the truth the mage had been evading the previous night—that rescuing Julie Salgado, while it might help their cause, wasn't their only priority.

"So we work on the Barrier?" Ines asked.

"Exactly." Shaw pointed at the laptop. "I've been having another look at your mother's notes on the Barrier. We need people and equipment before we can cast the magic to repair it. But more than that, we need information."

"What sort of information?"

"Have you studied much experimental theology?" Marklew asked.

"None," Ines replied.

"Ordinary theology?"

"Not my thing."

"You at least had religious education lessons at school?"

"Not since I reached sixth form." Ines looked at the coffee pot. It wasn't really to her tastes, but maybe she was going to need the caffeine. "And I didn't pay that much attention before."

"Then let's just call it the sort of information found in university libraries," Marklew said.

"Are you saying that I'm too stupid to understand?" Ines narrowed her eyes. If her parents had trusted her enough to tell her more about their work, then she might not have struggled so much when things had gone wrong.

"You're one of the smartest young people I've met," Shaw said. "But no one has time to learn about everything, and there would be a lot to teach you before what we're talking about has any meaning. It's abstract concepts about spells and reality, old reports of obscure incidents, a series of things your mother thought might be relevant but that she hadn't gotten to yet, or hadn't anticipated needing to know."

"Then let's go get some books," Ines said.

"First things first," Shaw said. "We need to talk about you."

The next hour felt like a long, drawn-out, and obscurely intentioned interview. Over the cooling piles of food, Shaw and Marklew asked Ines question after question about her life. Shaw made notes on the laptop. Marklew made more coffee and increasingly regular huffing sounds as the questions failed to draw out the answers he was looking for. Rumiel and Damon drifted in and out, grabbing food before retreating from a conversation they had no part in.

The questions started with Ines's religious education—what schools she'd attended, what her teachers had been like, what religions they had discussed, and how they had described them. From there, they got into what she had learned at home from her parents about the world of magic, angels, and demons, including the training they had provided so that she could protect herself. References to her brother and his gift for magic intrigued Marklew, and he perked up as he learned about Ines's complete lack of ability to handle the craft.

"Have you ever seen things happen the other way around?" he asked. "Spells reversing, or perhaps dissipating suddenly in your presence?"

"Magic works fine around me," Ines said. "Shaw has seen that firsthand. I just can't cast anything myself."

Expelling another deep huff of annoyance, Marklew sagged in his seat, his huge body slumping over a plate slick with breakfast grease.

"I'm at a loss," he said. "And a trifle embarrassed by it."

"Here's the thing." Shaw leaned forward. "Whatever's special about you, Ines, whatever lets you fight angels and demons like you have, that's important. If we're going to win, then we need to make use of it. It might even connect in with how Oldfield brought the barrier down and how we can repair it."

"So how do we find out what's special about me?" Ines asked.

"I don't know." Shaw shook her head, flopping hair revealing her scarred cheek. "So think about it, and if you have any ideas, however odd they sound, let me know."

* * *

The University of Durham, Ines learned, was spread across the town, occupying dozens of different buildings— some purpose built, some created by knocking together old terraces, and some historical buildings like the castle itself, which she was amazed to learn was now a college in which hundreds of students lived. Adjacent to the castle, on one side of the open green separating it from the cathedral, was one of the university's smaller libraries. So while Shaw took Damon and Rumiel with her to the main library, Ines accompanied Marklew to the heart of historic Durham.

"Ah, Palace Green," Marklew said as they strolled past the well-kept lawn that separated castle from cathedral. "How many wild adventures I had up here in my youth."

Ines glanced back and forth, her attention torn between the cathedral— even more spectacular up close—and the vicar's collar around Marklew's neck. Their host's appearance in that particular piece of clothing had clearly surprised Damon too. But there had been no chance to discuss the strange fact of this large, jovial gay man serving as a minister in a church still divided over questions of faith and sex.

The building they were walking towards was irregular looking. Made of the same yellowish stone as much of the city's other old architecture, one end of it looked a lot like a chapel, with its sloped roof and tall windows, while parts looked like fragments of a stately manor house or a flawed modern imitation of something ancient and venerable. Like her guide, it felt less like a coherent whole and more like an accumulation of pieces combined by proximity rather than design.

"I've arranged access to the cathedral archives as well," Marklew said as they approached the doors of the library. "But we'll have to wait for that, as they're not generally open to the public, and my friend isn't on duty until this afternoon. In the meantime, we should be able to find—"

"Wait." Ines grabbed his arm, stopping the large man's forward momentum through the ferocity of her grip. Peering through the glass of the library doors, she saw a man in a grey suit at the far end of the lobby, and a woman in matching clothes across the room from him. "Ministry mages. We should come back later."

"They might be friendly," Marklew said. "Let me go inside and see who—"

"Nobody friendly to us is going to be standing guard like that."

Turning to look around, Ines spotted two more grey-suited figures at a cafe table on the opposite side of the green. Another was emerging through the castle gates to their left, and one more stepped out onto the pavement between them and the cathedral.

"Ambush," she said. Thrusting her hand up her sleeve, she took a grip on the knife hidden there.

"Steady," Marklew said. "This isn't London—you can't pick a fight without drawing everyone's attention. If we're lucky, that's something they'll want to avoid."

With slow steps and wary glances all around, the two of them started walking back the way they had come, towards a short road between houses that led down into the town center. The mages at the cafe stood and walked quickly to intercept, while the others moved in behind them.

"All right, so maybe the subtlety won't last much longer." Marklew rolled his shoulders. "Wish I knew some damn magic right now."

"You don't?" Ines asked in incredulity. "But you were talking all about experimental theology and Ministry matters."

"I know the theory," Marklew said. "But I'm no mage, just a theological consultant."

Ines groaned. "This is bad. If they attack us with spells—"

As if to make her point, one of the mages ahead of them twitched his fingers, the air between them starting to shimmer. He stepped out into the road, blocking their path. There was no traffic to get in the way, and at a mystical gesture from his colleague, the few passing pedestrians turned, blank eyed, and walked stiffly back the way they had come.

"Now can I get my knife out?" Ines asked.

"It seems prudent," Marklew said.

The mage who had chased away the pedestrians waved his hand again. Ines felt numbness behind her eyes but shook it off.

"Won't work on someone who's aware of it, I'm afraid," Marklew called out. "Now, do you really want to make a scene?"

"Do you really want to resist?" the mage replied. "If you just come with us, this can all go easily."

Ines drew her knife and shifted into a fighting stance.

"Just try it," she said.

There was a crackle as the remaining mages wove their hands through the air, glowing clubs and shields appearing as if from nowhere. The leader wove a ball of something cold and blue between his palms.

"On my mark," he said.

"Mark." The voice came from between the stone gateposts of a house to Ines's left. The air rippled, and a woman in black trousers and T-shirt appeared. As she swung her arm, a magical club shot from her hand, colliding with the back of the head of the nearest mage.

Another black-clad figure leapt from a rooftop, landing lightly behind two of the mages. As they turned in amazement, he flung his arms wide, and sparks seemed to stream from between them. They hit the mages, who went flying back across the street.

A car screeched to a halt at the end of the short road. "Get in!" the driver yelled, flinging a door open.

Ines raced towards the car, Marklew thundering along behind her. One of the mages took a swing at her as she passed. She ducked beneath the blow and brought her knife up, catching him across the forearm. Blood flew, and she kept running, leaping in through the door and onto the backseat of the car. Marklew followed, slamming the door shut behind them.

As the engine roared and they raced away, Ines looked back. One of their rescuers shot into the air, up onto the rooftops and away, while the other strode back between the gateposts and vanished. The Ministry mages looked around in anger and bewilderment while blood ran onto the ancient cobbles.

CHAPTER 5
Rebel Alliance

Marklew showed every sign of delight at welcoming the new arrivals into his home. They were made comfortable with the same mixture of lively exclamations and heaps of refreshments that had greeted Ines and her travelling companions. While he didn't know any of them, he had heard of Hema Panesar, the woman who had led the rescue, and accepted without question their story of being rogue mages. Given the dramatic confrontation they had just been through, Ines was also inclined to believe them.

"I've never had a chance to explore the way magic connects in with Hindu theology," Marklew said as he roamed the living room, handing out Danish pastries and cups of coffee, offering sugar, milk, and whiskey to flavor the drinks. "You must sit down with me while you're here and let me pick your brain."

"I haven't been to temple since I was seven years old, Professor Marklew," Hema said. "I'm really not the girl for you."

"No one is the girl for me," Marklew said, winking at one of the male mages. "And call me Tim."

So Marklew was a professor as well as a priest. Ines found herself ever more curious about him.

"That applies to you too," he said, misreading the dazed expression on her face. "No more Mr. Marklew, or Doctor, or Professor, and certainly not Reverend. Here, have a donut."

A click and a creak from the hallway announced that the door was opening. Hema and her colleagues leapt to their feet, while Ines reached once more for her knife. In the silent moment that followed, a chill ran down her spine. What had become of her, that her first response to a surprise was to prepare to stab someone? How could she ever come back from a life like this?

"It's me and the boys," Shaw called from the hallway.

"I am hardly a boy," Rumiel declared. "I have lived through ages beyond your comprehension, seen suns rise and fall over—"

"Just get inside," Damon snapped. "The longer we stand out here, the more likely it is that Oldfield's agents will spot us."

Shaw smiled in delight as she came into the living room. She wrapped Hema up in a tight hug, and Ines was once again surprised at the adults around her. Where was the steely-eyed professional she was used to dealing with? When had grownups stopped being so simple to understand?

"I'm so glad you're here," Shaw said. "How did you find out?"

"Simms," Hema replied. "He's still out there recruiting, but we were his first stop."

By now, Marklew's living room was becoming crowded, but as he and Damon brought in stools from the kitchen and fetched tea and coffee, everyone found a place to sit. There were introductions, awkward shuffles for space, and the devouring of the remaining pastries. Hema and her companions explained how Simms, one of the mages from Manchester, had reached out to them to aid Shaw. More rebellious mages were being recruited, donning black as their new uniform to stand out against the grey suits. On their way into Durham, Jason, the driver and a specialist in sensing out magic, had noticed the disturbance brewing around Palace Green, and they had come to investigate.

When Hema was finished, Ines described the rescue from her side, and their failure to even enter the library, never mind visit the cathedral archives.

"We had more luck," Shaw said, opening a large bag that Rumiel had carried in. It contained a collection of books, some small and some large, some new and some looking nearly as old as the cathedral. "Everything we needed is here. I was able to nullify the security barriers long enough to bring it all out without drawing attention." She passed one of the older books carefully to Damon. "What do you think?"

He opened the leather-bound tome and carefully turned a stiff, yellowed page. Laying his hand against it with delicacy that made Ines smile, he pulled the watch from his pocket and began to chant. A small bubble of blood appeared at the corner of his mouth as he bit his lip, seeking a little pain to power his demonic magic. The sight of even such a small injury on him made Ines unhappy, but she sat still, letting him do his work.

A black cloud emerged from Damon's hand and settled across the page. When it dispersed, the paper was as crisply white as if it had just been made, the faded letters stood out boldly, and the crumbled edges of the page had been restored.

"It'll work," he said, nodding in satisfaction. "I should be able to make everything readable, however old and battered it's gotten. It'll show any notes people have made down the years, or codes that were written onto pages before the rest of the text was written around them. But it'll take time."

"Start with this." Shaw handed him a smaller tome. "But first, we need to talk strategy."

Looking around the room, she caught each of their eyes in turn, finally settling on Ines.

"This is yours to lead if you want," the mage said. "You've earned it."

Ines shook her head. Things were shifting so fast, she felt bewildered by it all. It had been one thing to lead two of her friends through the perils of Mancunian riots—trying to take charge of a room full of adults was another matter.

"All right, then." Shaw looked around the room again. "You all know what's happening. Most of you have seen the chaos the collapse of the barrier is bringing. The violence as demons prey on the worst in humanity. The angels turning people into blissed-out zombies or judging them for sins, real and imaginary. Elizabeth Oldfield brought that about. Now she and the angels of the Blazing Host are using it for their own agendas, while the demons go about whatever foulness they have planned." She glanced at Damon. "No offense."

"None taken," he said. "I plan on behaving foully myself once I'm old enough to drink—it's the British way."

"We have to restore the Barrier of Mercy to what it once was," Shaw said. "To stem the tide before things get any worse. To give humanity a chance to rebuild."

There were murmurs of agreement and nodding heads. The mages looked grimly determined, Marklew hopeful, Rumiel confident, and Damon intent upon his book. But in Ines, a doubtful thought stirred, a twinge of discomfort at a purpose that sounded so reasonable but hid something darker.

"I don't think this is about restoring what was there before," she said.

"Whyever not?" Marklew asked.

"Two reasons." Ines swallowed. Now everyone was looking at her, she felt nervous, her thoughts tying themselves into incomprehensible knots. She paused, trying to disentangle them enough to express herself, and then continued. "Firstly, there's all the damage that's been done while the Barrier was down. People killed. Lives ruined. Communities shattered. It's not enough to just stop any more damage happening and leave the world as it is—someone is going to have to make things better, and if we can, then that someone should be us.

"I don't understand a lot about the Barrier of Mercy. I'm not a mage or a demon or a theologian. I don't have a gift for these things. But even I can see that the Barrier is massively powerful, and that it touches every corner of the world. So if we're going to do something with it, then part of what we should do is use that power to undo the damage. To heal people's wounds and calm their spirits. To bring some unity out of this horror.

"I'm not saying we can undo all the harm that's been done. Short of turning back time, that would be impossible. But if we're going to tap into vast power, then we should do as much good as we can."

She flushed and looked down at her hands, caught in the headlights of their collective attention. She had been garbling it all, she was sure, talking too fast to get to the end, afraid that someone would tell her how wrong she was. But if they were going to shoot her idea down, then it was better to get it over and done with.

"Damn right, we should," Damon said, setting aside his book.

"Very well said, young lady." Marklew patted her on the shoulder.

To her amazement, she heard everyone in the room express their agreement.

"You said there were two reasons," Shaw said. "What's the other one?"

Her confidence boosted by their responses, Ines took a deep breath and prepared to plow on. She had thought that the other part might crash up against the realities of what was possible. This one would test the values of some people in the room.

"The way the Barrier was before, it wasn't good," Ines said. "It was tied into old allegiances—Heaven against Hell, the two pushing back and forth against each other, with Earth as a place for them to fight it out, grappling over souls. Even before the Barrier came down, angels and demons meddled in people's lives. The Barrier made them do it in hidden ways, but hiding a problem only lets it fester. And doing it that way bound everyone up into what they had been told they had to be. Rumiel was on the side of Michael, even though Michael is a murderer. Damon was expected to serve Hell. The Ministry treated the rest of humanity like sheep, to be watched over and kept uninformed.

"That should change. We should make a Barrier that does away with the old allegiances, that brings reality out into the light. If all of this isn't to be a meaningless waste of life, then it has to bring change."

"Yes!" Damon exclaimed.

"What you say has great merit," Rumiel agreed. "To be free to make our own choices, no matter our origin, would be a thing of worth."

He smiled at her, and she smiled back. If he was free from the obligations of the Heavenly Host, what might that mean for them?

"It's a noble sentiment, my dear," Marklew said. "But I'm not sure that such changes lie within the possibilities the Barrier holds."

Shaw nodded. "I don't know how much of that is tied into the Barrier, and how much is just the way people are."

Deflated, Ines sank back in her seat.

"We can try, though, can't we?" she asked.

"Look at us," Shaw replied. "Thanks to you, we've already broken the hold of old ways over us. We wouldn't be sitting in this room if we hadn't. If you say it's worth doing, then we'll give it the best try we can."

Again, there were murmurs of assent, and applause rippled through the room. Ines felt herself go red with a strange mixture of pride and embarrassment.

"Here," Marklew said, handing her a small glass of port. "You've earned it."

The drink was sweet, heady, and strange. It felt thicker on Ines's tongue than she had expected. She thought she liked it but wasn't completely sure.

"If we're going to do this, then it will take more than just us," Shaw said, all business. "We need angelic and demonic power to rebuild the Barrier, and just Rumiel and Damon may not be enough. On top of that, when the time comes, we'll need people to hold off Oldfield, Michael, and anyone else who objects while we cast the most difficult spell humans have ever undertaken.

"Murphy and Simms are gathering more mages, but we need others as well. There are people on every side of this who want to see the Barrier repaired, or at least to give Michael and the Ministry bloody noses. So let's get them on our side.

"Rumiel, try to think of who the friendly angels might be and how we can contact them. People who aren't aligned with Michael. People who would want to heal the world.

"Damon, like it or not, you're a big player in the demon world now. It's time to step up and use that authority to bring us back from the dark side.

"This isn't going to be easy. We're all going to have to work with people we've been taught to hate. But we can do it."

"Woohoo, time to talk with Dad," Damon said, his voice heavy with sarcasm. Then his frown lifted, and his voice brightened. "On the other hand, I love that we get to play at being the rebel alliance."

CHAPTER 6
What We Don't Know

Night had fallen over Durham, its black shroud calming the city and the world beyond. Ines sat on a wooden bench in Marklew's small backyard, between a pair of neatly trimmed potted shrubs with sweetly fragrant leaves. A line of light escaped from around the blinds in the kitchen window, its narrow glow hitting the bottom of the three steps from the back door. Other than that, the only light was the stars shining high above. It was a relief to just sit and stare at them, thinking about nothing but those distantly twinkling lights.

Ines wondered how often in the past people had looked up at that sky, with its bright points and its mass of darkness, and thought about demons and angels.

Had people in centuries past thought that those stars were angels themselves, watching over them? Had they looked up on cloudy nights, with all the light in the world ripped away, and wondered at what dark forces might descend? Had any encountered the creatures directly, as she had? Had their worlds also been shaken?

The muffled sound of a radio in the kitchen became louder as the door opened, spilling a wider beam of light down those steps. The radio had been on for most of the evening, as Marklew and Jason deftly tuned it from one crackly broadcast to another, picking up information from those stations still broadcasting across the country. Various factions were using the airwaves to send out their messages, and all appeared to be trying to block each other.

With Scotland such a short distance to the north, and her people apparently more united than those in England, the new Scottish government station had the strongest signal, carrying news not just from their country but from the rest of the world. There was talk of fresh warfare in Latin America, a coup in the Philippines, and pendulum-like swings back and forth between wild protest and brutal oppression in China.

Meanwhile, voices claiming to represent the British Parliament and the royalist army each used crackling, half-jammed stations to put forth claims about crimes and outrages by the other side. The only truth that could reliably be picked out was that there would be no compromise between these bitterly opposed factions.

Damon closed the door behind him. He came over to the bench and sat down beside Ines. Tentatively, he reached out and took hold of her hand, interlacing their fingers. Heart racing, she leaned her head against his shoulder, enjoying the moment while there was no one around to see.

"Are we all right?" he asked. "Before we left Manchester, I thought that maybe we were... that we had... that this was going somewhere. But now I feel like you're backing off."

"Everything's so busy," Ines said, looking for a way to avoid the truth without lying. "I can't think about this right now, and I don't want to have to answer other people's questions about it. I know it's not what you want, but can we please keep what's happened between us quiet for now? Nothing in front of the others."

"It's probably for the best," Damon said. "I wouldn't want to break hearts, and there are hundreds of young women breaking down my door for this prime piece of man flesh."

Ines laughed. "I'd break a few doors down for that."

"You see? It's madness."

He leaned in, and they kissed in the darkness beneath the stars. For a wonderful, lingering moment, Ines felt as though she had come home.

"Now excuse me," Damon said, pulling away. "I have to go find some demons to talk to."

"Now?" Ines asked. "At night?"

"It's the best time," Damon said. He squeezed her hand and then let it go. "Even if it's also the worst."

* * *

In daylight, it was harder to romanticize the view around the backyard. A concrete square a dozen feet across, hemmed in by crudely cemented brick walls, it was fundamentally an ugly space. Marklew's potted plants and wooden bench had been artfully placed to take off the rough edges, but there was only so much they could achieve.

But it was still the best place for what Shaw wanted to do.

"Again," she said from where she sat on the bench beside Ines.

Raising a club of pure magical power, Hema swung at Rumiel from left and then right. First, he parried a blow from each side with his sword, then he dodged them. Next, Hema changed the club, shifting the magic so that it became little more than a faint blue shimmering in the air. They went through the same succession of attacks and defense.

"That second one seemed to work better," Shaw said. "How did it feel to you, Rumiel?"

"More potent," the angel said. "On the first blow, it was as if it drew power from my sword. The unbalancing experience slowed my second counter."

"Good. Any edge we can find will be important when facing Michael." Shaw touched the scars on her face then dropped her hand into her lap. "You two go inside, find the other mages, and talk through as many spells as you can think of—not just the combat stuff the Ministry taught us all, but each of your specialties. Let's think about how we can use the flow of our own magic to take angels down. And Rumiel, tell them how you would fight back against each one. Let's look for anything the angels will have trouble countering."

"It is curiously satisfying," Rumiel said. "Not to fight, but to help others refine their own technique."

"Yeah, great," Hema said. "We'll make a leader of you yet. Now get inside—I want to make a cuppa before we start." As she passed the bench, she squeezed Shaw's shoulder and smiled at her. "You're doing great, Tamsin. Don't beat yourself up over imagined failings."

The kitchen door closed, leaving Ines and Shaw alone in the yard. The mage took a deep breath then turned to Ines.

"Your turn," she said.

"Me?" Ines asked, surprised. "How can I help come up with ways to fight angels?"

"That's not what I meant," Shaw said. "Though given your experience, I think you'll have a lot to contribute there later. No, what I want is to start testing your abilities and your nature. To get into what's so special that it let you achieve so much."

"Okay," Ines said. She felt as nervous as if she were about to take an exam. "Though I don't feel at all special."

"Rare words from a teenager."

Shaw knocked on the kitchen window, and a moment later, Jason stepped out to join them. This morning, he had gelled his blond hair up into spikes, a punky look that never would have been allowed when he was a suited Ministry man. It went well with the relaxed black outfits the rebel mages had chosen, and which Shaw had now adopted, borrowing clothes off Hema.

"We're going to start by using Jason's sensing abilities," Shaw said. "I'll throw bursts of magic at you, and he'll look to see what's happening. Are there any strange patterns or shifts in the way the magic works? Does it flow differently around you? That sort of thing."

"Is this going to hurt?" Ines asked, remembering the way Rumiel had flinched when Hema hit him in the shoulder.

"No, it won't be that focused," Shaw said. "But it might be unsettling. Feel free to close your eyes if that helps."

For the next hour, the garden was a haze of power. Shaw threw ever-growing waves of raw energy at Ines from every angle. Mostly it was all right, though there were times when Ines's skin crawled at the energy running across it, or when the power made her head spin. They had to stop when one particularly intense blast made her stagger and almost throw up. After that, Shaw lightened up in the power she was using, though her look of annoyance grew. She appeared almost as frustrated as Ines felt, with so much effort going into discovering nothing.

"I'm sorry," Jason said for what seemed like the millionth time. "I'm still not seeing anything unusual. The power runs over her just like it would any human. She's not shaping it, not absorbing it, not redirecting it. And I hope I'm not speaking out of turn here, but this can't be good for you, Ms. Shaw."

"What does he mean?" Ines asked.

"My natural power lies in nullifying the energies of others," Shaw said. "Projecting energy like this runs against what my body wants to do. But I've had years of Ministry training. I'm already used to using magic that doesn't suit me."

"So you've been doing some sort of magical contortions, and we still don't know what's happening with me?" Ines heard her voice rising but didn't care. "This is stupid. It's not fair. It's part of me. I should be able to work it out. Why can't I do that?"

"If we knew what was happening, maybe I could tell you," Shaw said, her tone soothing. She looked over at Jason. "My granddad always said that the world looked better across brown liquid. Let's put the kettle on and discuss other approaches. Ines, would you like a drink?"

"No." She crossed her arms and flung herself down on the bench. "I just want to be alone."

"Sorry," Jason said as the two mages headed indoors. "I'm sure we'll work something out."

"I'm not," Ines snapped.

Alone again, she watched little white clouds scud across a blue sky. She couldn't find peace in the simplicity of it all. She was too wound up from an hour of fruitless work. The more they tried to work out what was happening with her, the more desperately she wanted to know, and the more the frustration of not knowing ate away at her.

The door opened.

"I want to be alone," she said.

"Will even my company not comfort you?" Rumiel asked, closing the door behind him. The sunshine turned his hair into a golden halo, and his eyes sparkled with light.

"Probably not," Ines said, shuffling over so that he could sit beside her. "But you're welcome to try."

The bench creaked as Rumiel sat down, the muscles in the arm he leaned on bulging.

"All will be well," he said. "I am here for you."

He leaned in and planted a kiss on her lips. Ines felt her whole body tingle, and without thinking, she reached around to grab the back of his head, pulling him in closer for a wild, passionate moment. The sensation of him pressed against her was electrifying.

Remembering herself, she jerked back, pushing him away.

"Did I do that wrong?" Rumiel asked. "I have little experience at this."

"No, not wrong," Ines replied, caught between grinning and guilt. One bench, two boys. What was it about this place? "Definitely not wrong. It's just... This isn't a good time. We have a war to fight, or maybe to stop, and this is a big distraction."

"Distractions can be good." Rumiel took hold of her hand. "They can relieve the strains of hard times."

To Ines's relief, nobody was looking out at them from the kitchen. Still, she reluctantly drew her hand away from his.

"I need to stay focused," she said. "And I need everyone else to see that's what I'm doing."

"You are so good, Ines Salgado," Rumiel said with a wide smile. "Keeping up the morale of others."

"That's me." She forced a smile in return, guilt twisting more tightly in her gut. "All about the morale. So can you please keep quiet about the kisses and everything that's happened with us? And avoid doing it again when anyone might be around?"

"Of course." Rumiel stood. "As always, I shall be the perfect figure of righteousness. And now, I shall leave you, so none wonder what passes here."

The familiar sound of the kitchen door closing signaled that Ines was once again on her own. Frustrated in more ways than one, she sank her head into her hands, hoping that, for a while at least, the whole world might go away.

CHAPTER 7
The Bus to Bear Park

"What do you mean, you won't?" Shaw glared at Damon across the kitchen.

Caught between the two of them, Ines tried to back quietly out but instead knocked the dishes on the draining board. She froze, not wanting to draw any more attention.

"I think it's self-explanatory," Damon said coldly. "It was one thing to take on demonic magic. Sinking into their politics is too far."

"They could be fighting for us," Shaw said. "You said it yourself—all you have to do is accept your title as lord, and they'll do whatever you want."

"For now," Damon said. "But that title comes at a price. Part of that price is letting them dictate the terms of this."

"Terms where they do what we want."

"Terms where people do what I say because of who I was born, because of some title I've been given, not because I've asked them and they choose to side with me."

"You're rejecting the power because it's power?" Shaw looked baffled and more than a little angry.

"I'm refusing because of the sort of power it is."

Damon's fingers twitched, his pocket watch dancing back and forth across the back of his hand. After months spent so intensely in each other's company, Ines could see that he was as angry and frustrated as Shaw but keeping it inside.

The mage took two angry strides across the room and flung open the door. A sound like distant thunder reached them, despite the clear skies outside.

"You hear that?" she said. "That's artillery. Right now, some little village no one's ever heard of is a battlefield. It's being torn to shreds by Brancepeth-Holmes's lunatic royalists and the riled-up Scots. A few days from now, Bear Park won't be a village—it'll be a string of ruins and craters full of dead bodies. We can't afford to piss about, asking nicely, especially where demons are concerned. We need everything we have to end this."

"Someone always says that the end justifies the means." Damon's voice was low and menacing, his eyes going black as he let his power show. "But every moment is an end for someone, and every moment is a means towards the ones that follow. I won't continue a tradition I revile. There will be another way."

There was a knock. They all turned to see Jason standing in the door to the hallway, glancing nervously between them.

"Sorry to interrupt," he said, "but I think this might be urgent."

"Go ahead," Shaw said, still glaring at Damon. "Maybe whatever's happened now will bring Mr. Lorus to his senses."

"I picked up a message," Jason said. "Someone a couple of miles out of town using an old radio set. There are refugees in a church near Bear Park. They can't leave without risking being fired at, and they're afraid that if they stay, they might get hit by a stray shell. I was thinking we could maybe rescue them?"

"Come on," Ines said, glad of an excuse to draw her friends out of their argument. "Let's go remind ourselves that we're all the good guys."

* * *

There was no traffic on the roads out of Durham, and so they had a clear run out. They'd taken the bus from a depot on North Road, near the viaduct. Unlike a convoy of cars, it would let most of them fight off any attacks while Jason drove, and give them space for an unknown number of refugees.

Ines was amazed at the young mage's confidence behind the wheel. Even driving something so unwieldy, he flung them around corners and raced across junctions, his sensory magic giving him a better grasp of what was needed than any ordinary driver. It made for a bumpy ride, but one that was never as dangerous as it felt.

More unsettling were the figures that watched them as they passed. No humans showed their faces, but the ghostly shapes of demons hovered over every house and hedgerow, reaching out towards the travelers, hungry for the extra moment of rage or pain that would let them break through into the world. The nearby battle had drawn them from all over, like flies to a rotting corpse.

Ines sat near the front of the bus, kitchen knife strapped to her forearm, carrying a broom handle as an improvised club. Hopefully, it wouldn't come to a fight—she didn't fancy her chances against soldiers with guns. But better safe than sorry.

Behind her sat Rumiel and Damon, and beside her, Tania, one of the mages who had turned up over the past few days. Simms and Murphy were doing well at recruiting Ministry mages.

Short and bubbly, Tania specialized in plant magic, which could be used to turn trees and hedgerows into barricades if there was trouble.

"Nearly there," Jason said as they raced through an empty-looking village. "I'll drop you off then turn around in the car park. I don't think we're—" He frowned. "Something isn't right. I can't sense—"

Suddenly, the road in front of them heaved upwards, tarmac rising to block their path. Their brakes squealed, and the whole bus tipped, skidding to a halt just before they would have slammed into the blockade.

"It's an ambush!" Ines exclaimed, pointing out of the window.

Men and women in grey suits emerged from the terrace houses on either side of the road. Ministry mages, with clubs and shields of glowing magic in their hands. And in the middle of the street, blond hair pinned up above her elegant pinstripe suit, stood Elizabeth Oldfield.

"We have to get out of here," Damon said. He stood, one hand gripping a luggage rack, the other holding out his pocket watch.

"What of the people in that church?" Rumiel asked.

"If they exist, then I'm the prince of peace," Damon said. "It was a lie to draw us here."

Rumiel frowned. "We cannot know that for certain."

"Damon's right," Ines said. "Jason, drive!"

There was a crunch of gears as Jason flung the bus into reverse, backing right up to the terraces behind them. As he turned the wheel, windows smashed and mages leapt in, spells carrying them and sheltering them from the flying glass.

Swinging her broomstick, Ines ran back down the bus. Her shoulder slammed into the shield of the nearest mage, pain running down her arm, but she pushed on, knocking him to the ground. Before he could find his bearings, she kicked him in the crotch, causing him to grunt and curl up in pain.

To her right, Rumiel vaulted the seats, flaming sword stretched out in front of him. There was a flash of light as his weapon clashed with that carried by a mage. To the left, the air crackled as other attackers countered Damon's spells.

The bus jolted into movement. The ground shifting beneath them, the combatants went tumbling over each other. Ines's world became a confusing mass of flailing limbs, flashing magic, and bursts of pain. She caught a glimpse of Tania charging in with a shield raised, of Damon's fist flashing black as he threw a punch, and of Rumiel flying out through a broken window and then back in again.

A screech of rending metal and a scream of pain drew Ines's attention to the front of the bus. The driver's door had been ripped off, and the metal behind it was shredded as if attacked by a frenzied beast. In the gap, Elizabeth Oldfield hung from the outside of the speeding vehicle, clinging with one hand to the ceiling. Glowing claws extended from her other hand, and she was slashing at Jason, blood flying each time she caught his arm.

The bus veered wildly to one side as their driver lost control in his moment of pain, but then he righted them and kept them racing down the road.

Throwing off the mage she had been fighting, Ines ran towards the fight at the front. She flung her improvised club like a javelin, catching Oldfield in the shoulder, and for a moment, the woman ceased her attack while she struggled not to fall off.

Outside the bus, demons flocked in a growing crowd, the anger and pain letting them take their final step into the human world. Some were masses of spikes, others of tentacles. There were giant beetles and things like half-melted lizards.

"Damon, get them on our side!" Ines shouted, pointing at the foul creatures.

"I am Damon, son of Chron!" her friend shouted. "Will any of you aid us?"

"Are you a lord, Chron-spawn?" a thing with dozens of eyes said as it leaned in through the broken glass. "Do you bear right of command?"

As Damon hesitated, the creature cackled madly and flew away.

Drawing her knife, Ines clambered over the seats, trying to reach Oldfield.

"I know you, little Salgado," Oldfield yelled over the noises of the engine, demons, and magical combat. "You don't have the heart to use that on me."

"You think?" There was blood all over the seats, and Jason's skin was pale. Ines remembered her father lying injured in Manchester, the fight at the station there, and all the other times this woman's actions had put people around her at risk.

But she had never killed a human being, and she didn't plan to start now.

Lunging forward, she grabbed the arm with which Oldfield was clinging to the bus. Squeezing as tight as she could, she dug her nails in, for once wishing that they were long like those of other girls at school.

Oldfield flinched and flailed around with her other hand. Ines twisted to dodge the claws, but they caught Jason again, leaving a slash in the side of his neck.

Swinging with all her might, Ines punched Oldfield in the face. The mage yelped and let go of the bus, falling away to the side of the road.

They were nearly back in Durham, heading up a hill that would come out near the viaduct. Ines placed her hands against the wounds on Jason's neck and shoulder, pressing hard to staunch the flow of blood. Glancing back, she saw Rumiel fling the last mage out through the back window of the bus. Damon was crouched on the floor, and she couldn't see Tania.

"This," Jason whispered. "This will have to do."

The bus slowed.

"Keep going," Ines begged. "Just a little longer, and we'll be home. Someone there can help you. It'll be all right."

"Tired." Jason rolled his head to the side, his cold cheek pressing against the back of her hand. "Too tired."

His hands slipped from the steering wheel as the bus ground to a halt.

"No!" Ines scrambled around, unfastened his belt, and dragged him down into the street. Frantically, she tore off her T-shirt and shredded strips from it, wrapping improvised bandages around the mage's wounds. She pressed her fingers to his neck, but if there was a pulse, it was too weak to find. His chest had stopped moving, and no breath emerged from between his lips.

"Come on." She pressed his chest and blew into his mouth, desperately trying CPR. "Breathe."

"I am most sorry." With a firm hand, Rumiel pulled her away from the body. "It is too late. He is in Heaven now."

"No!" Ines slammed her fists against his chest. "It's not too late! It's not!"

Her protestations giving way to sobbing, she leaned against Rumiel's chest for a moment. As he moved to wrap his arms around her, she stepped back, looking over to see Damon descending from the bus. He was holding Tania in his arms, showing more strength than she'd thought he had. The air around the mage was a dark haze. Her arm was twisted strangely, and a long shard of glass was sticking up from her stomach.

"We have to get back," Damon said. "I don't know how long I can freeze time around her, and things will get bad quickly when that ends."

Rumiel scooped up Jason's body as if he were lifting a child. Grimly, they set off toward home.

CHAPTER 8
Counting the Cost

The house should have been livelier than it had been since Ines arrived. So many mages had arrived that the place was overcrowded. Marklew had gone out to find other homes where they could stay, safe places that would not draw Oldfield's attention. In the meantime, colleagues and old acquaintances filled his home from top to bottom.

But instead of the lively chatter of friends reunited, or the serious conversations of people preparing for action, there was a muted quiet, the silence broken only by whispers, murmurs, and footsteps.

A loud moan pierced the gloom, running down the stairs, along the hallway, and into the kitchen, where Ines sat with half a dozen others. Everybody's eyes turned to the ceiling, as if they might look up to see Tania's sickbed. But all they saw was textured plaster and cobwebs.

The moaning stopped.

Footsteps shook the ceiling and trudged down the stairs. Damon and Rumiel entered the already crowded kitchen. Both hung their heads and slumped their shoulders, as if they were dangling limply from invisible hooks, held from falling only by the tension of unseen wires. Damon poured himself a lukewarm cup of coffee from the pot in the middle of the table. Rumiel took a tub of ice cream from the freezer behind Ines, cast aside the lid, and started eating it, using his fingers as a spoon.

"How is she?" Ines asked. The way Tania had looked as Damon carried her back, followed by that terrible moan, made her fear more bad news.

"I have done what I can to heal her," Rumiel said. "But her injuries are grievous, and it may not be enough."

In a sudden burst of anger, he swung his fist against a cabinet door, reducing it to splinters.

"This is what I am for," he growled. "To save humanity and to protect it. What use am I like this?"

Ines laid a hand on his arm.

"It's not your fault," she said. "You've done what you could."

"Thank you." Rumiel squeezed her hand. Ines squeezed back briefly then let go. Damon was focused on his drink, only Shaw looking at the moment of casual intimacy.

"I've slowed the passage of time around the worst wounds," Damon said, eyes downcast, voice low. "But stabilizing her on the way back took most of my power."

"Go sleep," Shaw said. "Recover your energy. We'll need you later."

With a nod, Damon abandoned his coffee and headed back up the stairs.

"What now?" Hema asked, looking at Shaw. Everyone was avoiding looking out the window, fearful of seeing the body that lay out there, wrapped in bin bags, while they worked out what to do. It was no fate for anyone, let alone someone as bright and helpful as Jason had been.

"We'll try for Julie Salgado." Shaw looked over at Ines, who perked up at the mention of her mother's name. "If we're going to fend off Oldfield, then we need more power, and Julie's one of the best mages out there."

"Is a research mage really that useful in a fight?" Hema asked.

"Power is still power," Shaw replied. "We'll find a way to use it."

"So how do we rescue her?" Ines asked. "How can I help?"

"Jason got hold of plans to the main Ministry office," Shaw said. "Before..." She glanced towards the door, lips tight as she fought back whatever she was feeling. "Go find them, and gather whatever you think you'll need for a fight."

"We're tackling the main Ministry building?" Hema asked incredulously. "After what they just did to us?"

"They're licking their wounds too right now. It's the best chance we'll get."

As everyone got up from around the table, Hema touched Shaw's shoulder.

"Can we have a word outside?" she asked quietly.

The two of them stepped out into the yard.

Ines lingered, bending down and pretending to tie her shoelace while the others filed out of the room. Hidden from the window, she shuffled closer to the door, listening through a crack where it had been left ajar.

"This doesn't come from me," Hema said quietly. "You know I believe in you, Tamsin, as a leader and as a friend. But we're paying a high price to defy Oldfield. It's only natural for people to ask whether it's worth it. Whether we're really on the right path."

"I misjudged the mood," Shaw said. "Just how bad are things?"

"No one's talking about leaving yet, but it won't be much longer. And once people start leaving, it'll be harder to hold onto the new recruits as they arrive."

"Shit," Shaw said. "Okay, I'll think of something."

"I know you will," Hema replied.

There was a sound of movement, and Ines hurried away from the door. But as she left the kitchen, the two women still hadn't come back inside.

* * *

Eight of them went. Shaw, Hema, four other mages, Ines, and Rumiel. Damon was awake again by the time they'd left, but Shaw had insisted that he stay.

"There are two better things you can do for us," she said, staring him down in the hallway. "Get some demons on our side, and save your power to help the injured. Do those, and leave the raid to us."

Damon looked at Ines and tensed, ready for a moment of defiance, but at the shaking of her head, he subsided. Selfishly, Ines didn't want to be dealing with both him and Rumiel at once. Happily, Shaw was also right.

Shaw gave a speech before they left, standing in the hallway to be heard by the mages crammed into every corner of Marklew's house. She talked about strength, about unity, about their duty to ordinary people. Ines only half listened, her attention on the audience's reactions. It seemed to go down well, but there was still a listlessness among them that made her uneasy.

Then the eight of them headed out, creeping through Durham under cover of darkness. The streetlights had been switched off, and little light escaped from the windows of the houses they passed. It was strange, walking through a city so thoroughly cloaked in darkness. It made Ines uneasy, even as it aided them in their hidden approach to their target.

The university science site lay at the bottom of a hill, across a tight bend of the river from the old town with its cathedral and castle. It was hard to make out details of the buildings in the dark, but Ines got the impression that everything was straight edged and orderly, modern buildings of concrete and smooth brick.

"Here," Shaw hissed, gesturing towards a small door at the rear of one of the buildings. It wasn't hidden in the way of a trapdoor, but instead made to look unimportant, placed between recycling bins and a cycle rack. As someone shone the narrow beam of a flashlight, it revealed a solid door with no windows and a substantial lock.

Rumiel touched his hand to the door just above the handle. A glow emerged from around his fingers. The door melted, blobs of molten metal sizzling as they hit the ground. Then he grabbed the handle and swung it back.

This was the part of the attack they had been able to plan. One of the mages flung his hands forwards, and smoke billowed in through the doorway. As he rushed in, the smoke ran before him, so that it would cloud the view of those inside but not of their group.

Ines rushed in with the rest. They hit light switches as they ran, looking to see who or what was around them. Nobody moved in response to the intrusion, so they kept going, splitting up and running deeper into the building, down carpeted corridors, past glass-walled offices and meeting rooms, as well as laboratories full of arcane equipment.

At last, Ines reached the last room on her part of the search. Like all the others, its door was open, and it was empty—no people, no paperwork, not even a computer they could steal for intelligence.

When they met back in the first corridor, everyone had the same story.

"They must have guessed what we would do and cleared out," Shaw said.

"What about my mum?" Ines asked.

"Wherever they've gone, they took her," Shaw said. "I'm sorry."

A bright light flashed suddenly in the doorway through which they had entered. Ines turned in alarm to see a glowing figure in a white tracksuit, brass knuckles gleaming on his fists. He cast a predatory look across them as he shifted slowly from foot to foot.

"Sanctus." Rumiel almost spat the name of the other angel. "What do you want of this place?"

"I came to kill some mages," Sanctus replied. "These aren't the ones I expected, but slaying you and your pitiful little friend will add to my glory and to that of the Blazing Host."

With a roar, Rumiel flung himself at Sanctus. Wings burst from his back, beating so hard that the wind from them almost flung Ines from her feet. Slamming into Sanctus shoulder first, he hurtled out into the night, taking the other angel with him.

"Run!" he bellowed.

Ines and the mages ran after him. Their hands began to glow with magical power, while she reached for her substitute—the knife strapped to her arm. As she came out of the building, she was greeted not by the darkness of night but by the glow of half a dozen angels, their white clothes each from different eras in history, their flaming weapons matching their garb.

A shining woman with long golden hair and a white fur tunic swept out of the sky straight at Ines, an axe swinging in her hands. Ines flung herself to the ground, rolled aside, and came up just as the angel's weapon hit the concrete. Swinging as hard as she could, Ines slashed at the angel's arm with her knife, drawing a yell of pain and driving the angel back.

Not giving her opponent space, Ines leapt after her, and the startled angel backed into a bike shed, whose thin wall buckled as she hit it. Stabbing and slashing with as much speed and precision as she could, Ines forced her opponent to focus on dodging the blows. With her other hand, she reached around into the back of her belt, fingers closing around another knife. As the angel distractedly followed Ines's right hand, her left came around, plunging the blade into the angel's side.

With a scream, the angel took to the air, hurtling away with the knife still embedded in her chest.

Whirling around, Ines saw a mess of blazing power, magical weapons and spells clashing, filling the night like a terrifying fireworks display. In the center were Rumiel and Sanctus, beating at each other so hard and so fast that Ines had no idea who was winning.

A blow from Sanctus hit Rumiel squarely in the gut, and he sank to one knee. But as Sanctus raised his hands for a finishing blow, Rumiel swung upwards. Light exploded from his fist as he hit Sanctus in the jaw. The angel went flying, knocking two of his allies to the ground before crashing through the side of a building. He lay immobile as a section of wall gave way, collapsing on him.

Seeing their leader fall, the rest of the attackers backed away, taking to their wings as soon as they were clear of the mages.

"That was brilliant," Ines said, hurrying to Rumiel's side. "I can't believe you—"

Her excited words ran short as she saw his face. Those perfect features were screwed up in pain. One hand was clutched to his stomach, light seeming to bleed out between the fingers.

"I may..." He groaned, sinking to the ground. "I may need to rest now."

CHAPTER 9
The Triangle

There was one more surprise before they made it back to Marklew's. As they trudged through Durham, two mages carrying the unconscious Rumiel, a figure came blazing out of the sky and landed in front of them. Recognising the angel she had just fought, Ines prepared wearily for a rematch.

But the angel did not attack. Holding Ines's knife out on both of her hands, she knelt before Ines and the mages carrying Rumiel.

"Michael said that our victories would show our righteousness," she said. "But there have been no victories, nor actions worthy of right cause. So now I pledge to Rumiel and the Earthly Host."

Rumiel didn't stir from unconsciousness, much as Ines wished that he would. She could tell that some gesture was needed.

Laying her hand on the angel's head, she took the knife.

"Be one with the righteous," she said, trying her best to talk like Rumiel. "Be one of the Earthly Host."

* * *

"So that's what we're calling ourselves now?" Damon asked. "The Earthly Host? Because it sounds like the name of a bad Swedish metal band."

This time, they were meeting in the living room of Marklew's house. Several of the mages had moved quarters, going to stay with friends of Marklew's elsewhere in the neighborhood. That made enough space to stop everyone living on top of each other, while keeping them close at hand in case trouble started.

A familiar war council had formed, the same people being brought in by Shaw each time a decision was needed. Ines, Damon, Rumiel, Hema, Marklew, and Shaw. Enough viewpoints to get different ideas. Few enough to let everyone have their say and still reach a decision.

"The word earthly was meant to insult," a weary-looking Rumiel said with a scowl. "It indicates a lack of the heavenly. Michael's term for us, no doubt."

"I like it," Ines said. "After all, we're trying to look after people here on Earth instead of worrying about the needs of Heaven and Hell. It even makes us sound grounded."

"Grounded in terrible vocals and power chords," Damon said. "But if you like it, then I'll stop complaining."

Her heart lifting, Ines smiled at him.

It was a reminder that things weren't all bad, whatever the woes falling upon them. She had managed to rescue her father and protect her brother. They had sent the Ministry packing from their top base. And two of the hottest young men she knew were vying for her attention—the beautiful Rumiel and her smart, wonderful best friend. Lost in that thought, it took her a while to realize that the conversation had moved on.

"What do you think, Ines?" Shaw asked, snapping her back to reality.

"About what?" Ines asked. "Sorry, I was distracted."

Distracted by having Damon sitting on one side of her and Rumiel on the other, the three of them squeezed together on Marklew's sofa.

"About whom we reach out to," Shaw said. "Military backing could be a huge help in holding back the chaos while we rebuild the barrier. But whomever we reach out to, we end up offending the others, so we need to choose carefully."

"I don't like the royalists," Ines said. "That field marshal on the radio sounds terribly pompous, and some of the things he said were blatantly racist."

"At least we know who's in charge there," Marklew said. "Parliament don't have the same spokesman from one broadcast to the next, and have you noticed how they stopped referring to the prime minister?"

"The Scots, then?" Damon flicked his pocket watch back and forth in his hand. "They seem like an odd choice, given that we're still in England."

"They won at Bear Park," Hema said. "Militarily, we might as well be in Scotland now."

"And they still have their first minister running the show," Shaw said. "Things have been a little more stable north of the border."

"It sounds like the Scots are our best option, then," Ines said.

Damon and Rumiel nodded their support for her.

"I suppose the jocks will do," Marklew said with a shrug.

"Next, the demons," Shaw said.

All eyes turned to Damon. He stretched his legs out, black trousers and shirt making him look like one of the rebel mages, and let out a long breath.

"We've picked up a couple," he said. "Anyone with a hint of power in the demon realm will attract some of the more desperate sort. They're currently out around town, looking out for misery to feed off because I told them they couldn't have the pain of people here."

"I like not that they are with us," Rumiel said. "These creatures that feed off the pain of others."

"My magic feeds off pain too, and that's saved us more than once," Damon said. "Not that I like their company either, but I'll deal with them if it adds to Ines's little host."

"Thank you." Ines leaned in to whisper in his ear. "I know how uncomfortable all this is. I'm glad you're doing it."

"For you, anything," he whispered back.

Their faces were so close together it would have taken only the slightest movement to slip into a kiss. Ines felt her heart hammering and Damon's hand reaching for hers.

But Rumiel still sat at her other side, unaware of what had happened with her and Damon, and she still didn't know which she wanted. Hastily turning to face the rest of the room, she leaned forward, clasping her hands in front of her and away from Damon's.

"What's next?" she asked, looking to keep them all occupied.

"The Ministry," Shaw said. "For all the bad blood there is between us, most of the mages are good people, committed to keeping humanity safe. I'm going to call for a conclave."

"Do you think they'll come?" Hema sounded doubtful.

"What's a conclave?" Ines asked.

"It's an ancient tradition," Hema said. "A meeting of all the mages in an area, under a truce. By coming to the conclave, everyone agrees not to use their magic or to fight each other until an important issue has been discussed."

"So what, you think you can persuade Oldfield to stop fighting us?" Damon asked. "Because there's a body in the backyard that says she's too committed for that."

"That body was my friend!" Hema snapped. "Make a joke like that again, and I'll show you what I can do to demons."

She rose, hands crackling with magic.

"Calm," Shaw said, placing a hand on the other mage's shoulder.

The magic between Hema's hands began to dissipate.

"Don't you dare." Hema shrugged off Shaw's touch, and the magic flared again.

"He's just a child," Shaw said. "Remember that."

Tension tightened around Ines's heart as she watched the mages stare at each other.

"I need some fresh air." Hema strode out of the room.

Closing her eyes, Shaw took a deep breath and then another. The rest of them sat in silence, only Rumiel looking directly at her.

As the awkward pause grew, Marklew picked up a plate of cakes from the coffee table and waved it at the young people on the sofa, his jaw wobbling as if he wanted to say something but couldn't find the words. Only Rumiel seemed to have any appetite, grabbing a donut and wolfing it down.

"Truly, your foods are delicious," he announced. "Just to be human is to share in the second-greatest delight I have found on this world. The delight of sugary snacks. Of ice cream and cakes, chocolate and jelly beans. Of liquids strange in color yet delicious in their sweetness. Of a thousand wonders that dance upon the tongue."

"I've never heard junk food described in such poetic terms," Marklew said, grinning. "Yet you said this was the world's second-greatest delight—what could the first possibly be?"

"Ines," Rumiel said, beaming.

Beside him, she felt her heart glow with warmth. No one had ever said anything so beautiful about her.

"She is fair as the dawn sun," Rumiel said, turning to look at her. "Wise as the greatest scholar. Filled with charm such as none I have ever encountered. When I look upon her, I feel exalted like no other. When my lips—"

"The meeting!" Ines said, almost shouting in her rush to stop him mentioning their kiss on the train. "We should carry on with the meeting."

Her heart was still hammering, her face flushed. Glancing sidelong at the young men sitting to her left and right, she saw Rumiel still beaming, while Damon shot her a seriously questioning look.

"We're done," Shaw said.

Ines sighed with relief. Now all she had to do was extricate herself from between these two without either causing a fuss. Once she had more time, then she would make a choice between them. First to her feet, she was making for the door when Shaw called her name.

"Can you please stay," the mage said, "so we can talk about your mother?"

"Of course." Ines sat back down, feeling a buzz of excitement. Perhaps another rescue attempt was possible. Perhaps the mages had even heard from her mother.

Once the others had left, Shaw closed the door.

"What is it about Mum?" Ines asked. "Do you know where she is?"

"I lied," Shaw said, sitting back down in the chair opposite Ines. "And I think you know why."

Ines's spirits sank. Not just at discovering that there was no news, but at the certainty of what Shaw wanted to discuss.

"Is this about the boys?" Ines asked, staring down at her hands, twisting them around each other in agitation.

"Of course," Shaw said. "Now look at me."

Reluctantly, Ines met the other woman's gaze. She had expected to see judgement there. After all, she knew how this looked. She was a terrible person, leading Damon and Rumiel on. But she wanted them both. How was she meant to decide?

Instead of judgement, Shaw looked at her with concern.

"I can see what's going on," she said. "I understand. None of us are perfect. I've done things in the past I wasn't proud of because that was where my heart took me. Some of them weren't even about my heart, just my libido."

She paused and pressed her fingers against her temples, looking as strained as if she were trying to lift a car with her bare hands.

"This is why I'd make a terrible mother," she said. "I'm no good at this sort of talk.

"Look, I understand why you're attracted to both of those two. I can see why they're attracted to you. In normal circumstances, I'd tell you to take them both for a test drive then pick the one that gets your engine running. But these aren't normal circumstances, and as my granddad used to say, you can't stop for a cuppa when there's a dinosaur chasing you."

"Your granddad said some weird things," Ines said.

"I think it was deliberate. He liked to keep people on their toes." Shaw smiled and shook her head. "I wish he were here now. He did a far better job of being minister than Oldfield."

Ines blinked in surprise. She hadn't realized that Shaw, like her, came from a family of mages.

"You're doing a pretty good job of it yourself," she said.

"Huh." Shaw's smile widened. "I wasn't thinking of myself as the minister, but I suppose that, for our side, I am." Her expression went serious again. "Enough distractions. You can't keep playing those two young men. They're among our most important assets, they have a history of conflict with each other, and there's too much potential for this to go wrong. Pick one and be honest with the other, or back off from them both. Understand?"

Guilt twisting at her guts, Ines nodded. The hurt she could cause the two people closest to her was bad enough—she hadn't even thought about how it could affect others. What they were fighting for was too important for her to let her heart—or, as Shaw said, her libido—get in the way.

She didn't know what she would decide, but she had to do it fast.

CHAPTER 10
Conclave

"This isn't about Oldfield," Shaw said, raising her voice to be heard over the car's engine as they headed out into County Durham. Behind them, a convoy stretched out along the road, the mages of the Earthly Host following the pull of the magical beacon at the conclave site. "But we need her to think that it is. I'll be playing to the crowd, trying to win her mages around to our side, but I need you to do your part too. Work the room. Talk with people. Find any that might be sympathetic. Sow seeds of doubt if you can."

"Will there be some sort of vote?" Ines asked from the backseat. Outside the window, the hills were broken up by dry stone walls, trees, and occasional houses.

"That's not how it works," Hema replied from the driver's seat. "Sometimes there's an attempt to reach a decision by consensus, but usually it's just about opening up a dialogue, easing relations so that the big decisions can be made later."

"Historically, mages used to be power-grabbing sorts," Shaw explained. "They didn't like making decisions in the open, never mind by a vote."

Turning off the road, they headed through the gates of a stately home. The driveway was flanked by rows of oaks, leading up to a wide gravel turning circle between the wings of the house itself. Hema drove them right to the foot of the main entrance steps and switched off the engine, so that the car carrying Shaw took prime parking position.

"Let's be a little more subtle once we're inside," Shaw said.

They got out and followed her up the steps. Hostile figures in grey suits stared at them from every window of the building. Above the entrance, a pair of stone lions flanked a carved shield, their claws bared.

"I don't think Oldfield's being subtle," Hema said.

Even as the rest of the Earthly Host mages parked and formed up behind them, Ines couldn't shake off a feeling of intense menace. She wished that they could have brought Rumiel and Damon in case things went wrong. But Rumiel was still too badly hurt to fight, no matter what he said, and the rules of the conclave banned all supernatural beings from entering.

A sturdy oak door reinforced with ancient nails swung open in front of them. Ines strode through as confidently as she could, she and Hema walking on either side of and slightly behind Shaw, like bodyguards for an important dignitary.

The entrance hall had a floor of checkerboard tiles, wood-paneled walls, and tapestries hanging between the leaded windows. At the back, a pair of staircases swept up to a mezzanine. Between the staircases, another large door led into a grand-looking room.

Walking through that door, they found themselves in a large square space with a chandelier hanging over the center. Rows of chairs ran around the room. Some of them were antiques, clearly dragged from elsewhere in the house. Others were cheap plastic seats that looked as if they'd been taken from local schools or cafes. The grandest chair sat in the front row opposite the door, its high back and sides covered with cushioned red velvet. In it sat the sternly regal figure of Elizabeth Oldfield.

"Mistress Shaw," she said, not rising as they came in.

"Mistress Oldfield." Shaw walked to the center of the room and stood, arms folded, as she intoned words of ancient ritual. "By right of puissance and of rank, by staff and book, by oak and steel, I call upon the right of conclave."

"By all our art and all our skill, I accept," Oldfield replied.

The seats were filling up fast, mages of both sides looking to get the best views. The Earthly Host sat behind Shaw, flanking the open space between the center and the door. Some of those who came in aligned themselves firmly with

Oldfield—more than had come with the rebels. But the largest number of mages sat to either side. More people than Ines had expected remained unaligned. Perhaps there was hope here.

Taking a seat near the door, from which she could see everyone, she looked around. Several more mages had joined their group since they'd arrived, among them Simms and Murphy, the two who had been out recruiting. If they weren't still on that mission, perhaps they had reached everybody they could. Perhaps this was the whole of Britain's magery, and today would be decisive.

Or perhaps they had just run out of friends. After everything that had happened, it was hard to stay positive.

Another mage caught Ines's attention. Walking in with a group of Oldfield loyalists, he had a twitchy way of walking. As he passed Ines, he turned his gaze briefly but intently upon her. Detaching from the rest of his group, he slid quietly in among the unaligned mages, taking a seat near the back. He was not the only one among them still wearing his grey suit, yet she couldn't help thinking that it suited him too well, almost matching his sickly skin. His uneasy demeanor set Ines on edge. He was up to something.

The meeting began with speeches from Shaw and Oldfield, each explaining their views of what was happening, each attacking the other's behavior. Oldfield was icy cold, Shaw calm and reasonable, neither unleashing the fire of emotions evident behind their words.

After a short while, Ines looked over and saw that the suspicious grey mage had gone from his seat. Scanning the room, she could see no sign of him.

As quietly as she could, she walked out of the meeting. She wouldn't put it past Oldfield to set up some sort of trap for after the conclave, once it was just inside the rules. Or perhaps she had set an agent to track them to their base. Either way, Ines was intent on stopping it.

No one was visible in the entrance hall, but she heard a creaking from the mezzanine above. With swift, silent footsteps, she stalked up the stairs, fists at the ready. But when she got to the top, there was no sign of the mage—just a wooden handrail to stop people falling off the edge and a couple of statues casting long shadows against the wood panelling.

She turned, looking through a doorway to one of the upper hallways.

"Got you alone at last," a sibilant voice said behind her.

Spinning around, Ines saw the mage emerge like mist from the shadow behind one of the statues. She lunged forwards, grabbing him by the lapels and slamming him up against the wall.

"No," she growled. "I've got you, and whatever you were planning, it's over."

His eyes went wide. He raised his hands in panicked surrender.

"What are you doing?" he hissed. "They'll hear you."

"They'll hear you, more like," Ines said, pulling back her fist.

"Please, I have information for you." Slowly lowering his hand, he pulled a memory stick from his breast pocket. "About dealing with the Barrier. Your mother found references in Crabtree's Compendium and slipped them to me."

"You're on our side?" Ines asked, lowering her fist.

"I'm on any side that won't destroy us all," the mage said. "But please, we have to leave now. Oldfield can't be trusted. She's going to break the oath of conclave."

Floorboards creaked again, and Ines spun around to see three mages in grey emerging from the landing doorway, hands out and twitching as they prepared spells.

"That's enough from you, Scollins," the lead mage said. "If you and Salgado's whelp want to live through this, then you'll both reach for the ceiling."

Rage boiled inside Ines. This was meant to be a safe meeting. They had trusted Oldfield, and so walked into an ambush.

There was a clatter as the memory stick fell to the floor and Scollins raised his hands.

"You too, kid," the man said.

Ines leapt. Grabbing hold of the wooden rail with one hand, she vaulted over and swung around. Catching the edge of the mezzanine floor with her other hand, she released the rail and let her momentum carry her around. As she swung beneath the mezzanine, she let go, hurtling across the end of the entrance hall and into the meeting room. Her ankle buckled painfully beneath her as she landed, sinking into a crouch.

"It's a trap!" she shouted.

There was half a second of calm while her words sank in. She saw Shaw's expression shift from confusion, through anger, to grim determination. Then all hell broke loose.

Behind Ines, there was a crackle and a scream, and Scollins fell over the edge of the mezzanine, his body engulfed in flames. In the meeting room, every mage leapt to their feet.

In the kind of unison only born from planning, the mages behind Oldfield began flinging blasts of magic at Shaw. She spread her arms wide, the air in front of her became a grey haze, and the blasts vanished as they hit.

"We're outnumbered," she yelled. "Pull back and get out."

There was no panic amid the Earthly Host, but there was speed. In an instant, half of them had protective spells up around them. Some flew into the air on magical winds. Others gained sudden strength and, flinging more vulnerable companions over their shoulders, raced for the door. All the while, Shaw maintained her barrier while backing towards the exit.

Remembering the men who had attacked her and Scollins, Ines ran back out of the room, her twisted ankle sending spasms of pain up her leg. She couldn't leave those men to attack Shaw from behind.

Sure enough, the three men were stalking towards her, ignoring the mages fleeing past them. Flames leapt from the leader's hands, while the men behind him bulged with unexpected muscle. Against mages, getting up close was usually to Ines's advantage. In the face of these three, all her usual options vanished. Her instincts told her to run away, but instead, she ran forwards, ready to use the only weapon she had—being small.

One of the muscled mages came at her first. As he lunged at her, she leapt off her good foot. Just avoiding his grasp, she used his shoulder as a vaulting horse to propel herself at her other muscular opponent. Surprise crossed his face for a brief moment before she slammed into him, fingers first, gouging at his eyes. He staggered back, screeching.

She dropped to the floor at the foot of a staircase and tried to turn, but her ankle gave way, and she fell.

The other two loomed over her.

"Get ready to burn, little girl," the leader said, a glint of sadistic madness in his eyes.

As if from nowhere, Hema stepped off the bottom step, a magical club in her hand. Her first blow hit the fire mage on the back of the head, and he fell like a sack of potatoes. The other mage turned just in time for her second blow to hit him in the face. Blood spurted from the ruin of his nose as he collapsed.

"Come on." Hema dragged Ines to her feet, and they dashed out of the building. In the driveway, cars were racing away, the Earthly Host fleeing while Shaw stood by the last car, her shield spread out above them. Her teeth were gritted, and sweat poured down her face.

Ines and Hema rushed down the steps and through the magical shield. As Hema slid into the driver's seat and started the engine, Elizabeth Oldfield came out on the steps behind them. She raised her hands, and the two lions above the doorway sprang into life, landing with heavy thuds on either side of her.

"Kill," she purred.

The creatures bounded down, one ahead of the other. Shaw's eyes went wide as the first one leapt. As it collided with her shield, the magic vanished, and it went still. But it was still a huge lump of stone, a lump that hit Shaw straight in the chest. She fell back, the statue on top of her, with a sickening crunch.

The shield collapsed. The other lion leapt. Without pausing to think, Ines leapt too, slamming into it from the side. It was exactly like hitting a brick wall, but it did the job. She knocked the beast just far enough off its path, and it landed next to Shaw, not on her. The mage stretched out her fingers and touched the creature's paw, and it too turned back to motionless stone.

Once again flinging her whole body into it, Ines rolled aside the statue pinning Shaw. The look on the mage's face and the blood running from the corner of her mouth made Ines afraid to move her. But she was even more afraid of leaving her here for Oldfield.

With the last of her strength, she lifted Shaw into the backseat of the car and scrambled in after her. Before she could even close the door, Hema hit the accelerator, and they raced off down the drive.

Behind them, grey-clad mages came streaming out of the house, flinging their last futile blasts of magic after them.

In the backseat, blood bubbled between Shaw's lips. Her eyes rolled back in her head, and she went limp.

"No!" Hema exclaimed from the front seat. "Please, no!"

Pressing her fingers to Shaw's neck, Ines felt a wave of relief.

There was still a pulse.

CHAPTER 11
No Explanations

The smell of burnt rubber surrounded the car as they skidded to a halt in the hospital car park. Leaving the keys in the ignition, Hema leapt out and flung the back door open.

"Carefully," Ines said. "Her ribs are broken, and I think there's something wrong with her lungs."

Together, they lifted Shaw out of the car. Her breath was a terrifying sound, half rasping, half gurgling, and blood painted her lips.

Glass doors hissed open on the other side of the ambulance bay. A doctor peered out, cautiously at first. As he caught a glimpse of Shaw, he shouted to someone behind him, and a few seconds later, three people in scrubs wheeled a hospital bed out of the building.

"One, two, three, lift!" the doctor said. Swiftly and smoothly, they raised Shaw onto the trolley. Then they raced through the doors, the doctor shouting for things that Ines had only heard of on medical dramas.

"What happened to her?" the doctor asked. "If you can't explain it, then don't try—we've gotten used to that."

"A statue fell on her," Ines said, thinking fast.

"Saner than most of this week," the doctor said then immediately grimaced. "Sorry, I'm dog tired—tact's going out the window."

Ines wasn't surprised. The doctor's eyes were bloodshot, and bags had formed beneath them. Several days' worth of stubble protruded from a head that looked as though it was normally shaved smooth. She was so relieved that the hospital was still running, she wasn't going to complain about the manners of the staff.

"Can you help her?" Hema asked anxiously.

"I hope so."

The trolley disappeared into an operating room, where half a dozen figures in full scrubs and surgical masks stood ready for action. As the doors slammed shut, closing out Hema, Ines, and the doctor, he turned to look at them.

"Did a statue fall on you too?" he asked, pointing at the angry bruising that covered Ines's arm below the sleeve of her T-shirt.

They glanced at each other. From what Shaw had said, the mages used to use their own doctors, so they didn't have to explain injuries away. This was clearly new territory for Hema as well as Ines.

"Never mind," the doctor said. "I've heard enough mad shit and bad intentions this week not to want to hear any more. Let's just get you patched up."

He led them to a bed in the corner of the accident and emergency ward. The place was a hive of activity, packed full of patients and with medical professionals constantly hurrying back and forth.

"I wasn't sure there would be anyone here," Ines said.

"It's the best staffed we've been in years," the doctor replied, donning his stethoscope. "When the world falls apart, every medic worth their salt wants to save it. There's something comforting about the camaraderie. Now stop talking and take a deep breath."

Half an hour later, Ines's sprained ankle was strapped up and her shoulder in a sling. The bruises from shoulder-barging the statue were so severe that the doctor didn't want her using it until he could run more tests, and there was a long queue for that.

"I can't make you stay," he said, once he'd finished checking them both over. "But if you need that arm for anything, then you should get it properly seen to."

Then he was gone, off to deal with the next arrival.

"We need to find out what's happening," Ines said. "Check where everyone's at."

Hema nodded but didn't look keen. She glanced down the corridor towards the operating rooms.

"There's nothing you can do for her," Ines said, seeing the other woman's emotional pain. Ines knew that she wasn't good with this stuff, but she wasn't going to leave Oldfield free to act as she saw fit. Not after this. "I can't leave until I've had x-rays, and anyway, I can't drive. You need to go back to Marklew's and find out if everyone got home."

"You're right," Hema said. "Make sure they take care of her. I'll be back when I can."

* * *

By the time Hema returned, Ines had been through what felt like dozens of tests, with the doctors eventually concluding that she was just badly bruised. The sling was gone, and pain-killers had reduced the ache filling that whole side of her body.

Shaw was out of surgery but not conscious. Ines sat by her bed, watching the pipes dripping blood and nutrients back into her, listening to the steady beep of the machine monitoring her friend's vital signs.

That was a strange thought in itself—that this woman, so much older and more mature than her, so much more skilled and decisive, was now her friend. Less than three months ago, they had been fighting each other on the streets of London, and now she would follow Shaw to Hell and back if the mage said they needed to go.

All of which just made it more terrible to see her like this, battered and helpless in a hospital bed. What if Oldfield found out that she was here and came for her? Or the angels did? Or the demons?

When Hema walked up to the bed, Ines assumed that her grim expression was all about Shaw. But as Hema took the other mage's hand, patting the back of it reassuringly, a smile touched her lips.

"She's alive," she said softly.

"They say she'll recover," Ines said, leaving off the all-important "probably" the doctor had included in the sentence. "She just needs time and care."

"Thank all the gods," Hema said, sinking into a chair. "At last, some good news."

Ines's stomach sank at those words.

"How bad is it?" she asked.

"We didn't lose anyone," Hema said. "Tamsin saw to that. But a lot of people are nervous now. Some are staying in their safe houses, refusing to come and meet at Marklew's. I think a couple of them have gone. Some are more determined than ever, but their tough talk is only alienating the waverers."

She brushed back her black hair, tying it more tightly behind her head. Next to her, Shaw's monitor kept beeping.

"That's not even all of it," Hema continued. "That angel who decided to follow you, she's worried that this is some sort of judgement upon our side. I think she might flip again. Most of the demons have gone, and Damon spent half the night persuading the last two to stay.

"For all the progress we've made, it feels like this has set us back even further. Now we have to claw back the ground we've lost."

"No," Ines said. She wasn't going to let it be that way. She couldn't. She didn't have the energy to start over from scratch. Even admitting a backwards step felt like a defeat. "No repeating what it's taken us so long to achieve. We're still ahead of where we were. We can find a way to keep moving forwards."

Suddenly, the beeping of the monitor changed. The steady beeping grew faster then turned into a long, drawn-out electronic tone, a sound TV had taught Ines to associate with terror.

Leaping to their feet, she and Hema cried out in unison.

"Doctor!"

Medical staff raced over, shoving them aside to get through. The doctor they'd met earlier took the lead as a nurse raced up with a defibrillator. Ines's heart pounded, and she felt as if she would vomit as he pressed the paddles together and then touched them to her friend. Shaw jolted and flopped back down.

The monitor returned to its steady beep, but the taste of bile clung to Ines's throat.

* * *

A small group had come up from town. The doctors had let them occupy a waiting room while they lurked around for more news of Shaw. No one had asked why they needed this space to themselves. The doctors and nurses were too busy to care. And so they waited, sitting on slightly stained sofas beneath white walls and crowded notice boards, reading leaflets on diseases and hoping for something to change.

"They say she's out of the worst," Ines said as she came into the room, offering the words like a life raft on a stormy sea. Just saying them made her feel better, and she saw the spirits of the others rise. Marklew took Hema's hand with a smile. Damon and Rumiel looked at each other in relief.

"What now?" Damon asked.

"I don't know," Ines admitted, slumping onto a couch. As her legs sprawled out in front of her, she noticed how filthy her jogging trousers had become, the loose material covered in mud, soot, and stains. It was a strange thing to notice, but then it was a strange moment. She felt as though she were watching her life from a distance, floating a few inches away from her body. "We press on, I suppose. Try to fix the barrier. That's what it's all about, right?"

"On that subject," Marklew said, "I have some ideas."

"I didn't think this was your field," Hema said, looking at him quizzically.

"I've always been something of a polymath," Marklew said proudly. "Some might say a prodigy, though humility bars me from repeating such a boast. Since you lot started turning up, I've been reading about it, and I think I'm getting the hang of this business."

"I thought this was specialist stuff," Damon said. "Isn't that why we needed Ines's mum's expertise?"

"Well, yes," Marklew admitted. "But she's given us a nudge in the right direction."

"You've heard from her?" Now Ines was on the edge of her seat.

"No, but you have," Marklew said. "Hema told me about your encounter with Scollins, the poor chap, and the notes he tried to pass to you. So last night I pulled out my own copy of *Crabtree's Compendium of Magical Barriers, Wards and Protections*—a most tedious and pompous tome, I should add—and did some reading. Then I looked through the materials we got from the library and found some articles your mother wrote

S.A. Beck

based on Crabtree. We might not have her latest findings, but I think we have enough to build upon her work."

Suddenly, they were all smiling again, leaning forward and waiting to hear what he had to say.

"I'll save the details for later," Marklew said. "But there are a few practicalities to consider. Firstly, time and place. We need somewhere powerful, and at the most powerful time of day. The cathedral would be perfect. It's just oozing magic, though even in this chaos, that might be hard to arrange.

"Sunrise or sunset would be best. The cusp of day and night doesn't matter in itself—after all, it's always midday somewhere. But the notice people pay to those times, the way they've regulated lives down the millennia, have invested them with power.

"As for the how, that's the interesting bit. Traditionally, the Barrier was built out of angelic power. Anything done by humans is going to need magecraft, so we'll be throwing that in too. But if we really want to rebalance the world as you suggested, if we want to make things different, then we should put in

139

demon magic too. By balancing those three forces, we might stand a chance of making something genuinely new."

He sat back, smiling. Hema and Damon started asking questions, things about magical theory that Ines didn't understand.

She didn't need to understand them. What mattered to her was that they had a direction to go in, even if they didn't have someone to lead them there.

Thinking of that brought fear for Shaw swelling back up. Hot on its heels was a memory of the fighting at the conclave. Of Oldfield's treachery and her attempt to kill them. Of all the things the minister had done. Of the harm she had brought down upon Ines's friends, her family, and her world.

They might not have Shaw to lead them anymore, but Ines had something to give her direction, and that was fury.

CHAPTER 12
Fractured Alliance

Making a decision was one thing, acting on it another. Marklew's plan for how to rebuild the barrier seemed solid, and everyone who heard it agreed that they should follow it. But that was as far as the conversation went. Having picked a way to act, no one seemed willing to push things forward.

It wasn't just that they lacked a leader, though that was important. It was that no one wanted to step up and take Shaw's role. To take charge of the Earthly Host, or even to encourage someone else to take the role, was to accept that Shaw was no longer in charge, to acknowledge that they had lost her. It was a step that no one, least of all Ines, was willing to take.

They drifted around the house, picking over details of the plan, occasionally going to talk to the mages in the other houses. Active but not purposeful. Thinking about where they were going but not steering their way there.

It was a knocking on the front door that finally pushed them to make a decision. As Ines opened the door, she was glad of the knife clutched behind her back. This was exactly the trouble she had expected—half a dozen mages, all in the grey suits of the Ministry.

"Tell Oldfield from me, if she wants to take us out, then she'll need more than just you six," she said, stepping back into a fighting stance. "There are plenty of us here, angels and demons as well as mages, and we won't go down without a fight."

She puffed herself up, trying to look convinced by her own half-truths. The only angels on their side had been missing since lunchtime, when Rumiel took Helda out to find good works they could do, intent on convincing her to stay on their side. The demons were skulking in the attic, waiting for someone to start giving them commands. As for the mages, she feared that, in their present state, some were as likely to run as to fight.

But she herself was burning with undirected rage, and if Oldfield's lackeys wanted a fight, then she would give them one.

"We weren't sent by Elizabeth," the leading mage said. His eyes twitched behind small round glasses, and he clutched his hands together anxiously in front of him. "But I spoke with Simms before, and he hinted that you were around here somewhere, and..."

His voice trailed off. Peering more closely at the others, Ines recognized some faces. At least two of them had been sitting at the edges of the conclave, in the middle seats of the unaligned mages. One had been sitting at the edges of Oldfield's group but hadn't joined in when they started attacking Shaw.

"What happened at the conclave wasn't right," that mage said, her gaze downcast, her brunette bob sheltering her face. "It was a betrayal of what we stand for."

"That's why we're here," the first mage said. "We want to work for Tamsin. That is, for Minister Shaw."

"Minister Shaw?" Ines said, lowering her knife. "I'm not sure she's been made minister. I'm not sure who would even make the appointment."

"The gathered mages would," Hema said from behind her. She had appeared in the doorway to the living room, face haggard and eyes bloodshot from lack of sleep, but with an energy about her that Ines hadn't seen since the hospital. "And it looks like they might be making a change at the top."

She ushered the new arrivals into the living room, and Ines followed, curious to hear more.

"It's not just us," the mage with the glasses said. "There's a whole group waiting at a hotel on the motorway and some more hiding out at a farm. I'm sure there will be others too, ones who are too scared to come forward yet."

He looked around the room.

"Is Tamsin here?" he asked.

Hema hid her feelings well—better than Ines thought she could have done.

"You must be thirsty," Hema said. "Ines and I will fetch some refreshments, then we can talk."

As the two of them left the room, Hema closed the door. She did the same as they entered the kitchen, putting as many barriers as she could between their conversation and their new guests.

"What do I tell them?" she asked quietly, taking the kettle to the sink.

"That you're in charge," Ines replied, going to fetch mugs and teabags. "After Shaw, you're the one the others listen to most."

"I can't do it," Hema said, shaking her head. "I'm good with small groups, but I clam up under this sort of pressure."

"You can do it," Ines said. "I've seen you take charge."

"Even if I could, it wouldn't work. Two of those guys in the living room outrank me, and they won't be the only ones. They're not going to listen to a team manager from the training department."

"Who else is there?"

"I don't know." Hema opened a cupboard and went rummaging around in Marklew's supplies of cakes and cookies. "Maybe one of them?"

"No." Ines took Hema's shoulder, drawing her out of the cupboard and closing its door, forcing the mage to meet her gaze. "We haven't worked with them. They haven't been through what we have. For all we know, some of them could be Oldfield's spies. It has to be someone who was committed to this before, someone we know we can trust."

"Then I really don't know." Hema turned away, returning to the boiling kettle.

Picking up a packet of biscuits, Ines threw it up and down in her hand, using the simple movement to calm herself. Her anger at Oldfield was seeping over into all her other thoughts, clouding her responses to those around her. She could feel it twisting her frustration at Hema's unwillingness to lead, turning that feeling into resentment towards the mage. Everything in her life was being poisoned by what the minister had done.

Clearing her mind, she let the rhythm of the throwing take over, becoming something hypnotic. Focusing on that one movement, she let go of the worries that assailed her, until only the most important thought remained.

They needed someone to take charge. She was going to find that person.

The back door opened, thudding against the wall as Rumiel and Helda strode in. Both angels were glowing. Rumiel crossed the room in three strides and swept Ines up in a hug.

"It feels good to be out there, doing righteous work," he said. "We saved three children from a car crash, stopped two fights, and put out a fire."

Gently prising herself out of his arms, Ines turned to Helda.

"Do you feel better now?" she asked.

"Indeed," the angel replied. "Yet still I struggle with a lack of certainty, of true purpose to our actions. It may make me sound like a wretch still in thrall to Michael, but I wish for leadership, for a strong hand to guide us."

"Ines, you should lead us!" Rumiel declared, laying his hands on her shoulders. "You are strong, wise, and courageous. All here respect you."

"You're not thinking with your head," Ines said, again ducking out of his affectionate grip. "I'm just a teenager. I can't lead an army of adults, angels, and demons."

"He's right," Hema said, realization spreading across her face. "You're the perfect choice. You led your friends before. You're not from the Ministry, so it doesn't matter what rank you have there."

"And it is to you that I swore my allegiance!" Helda said excitedly. "Yes, you are the leader we need!"

"No." Ines backed away from them into the corner of the room. The pressure of their eagerness was like a weight bearing down upon her. She didn't want this responsibility. She had already done more than she ever had before. "Find someone else, someone who knows what they're doing."

"You know what you're doing," Rumiel said.

"No, I don't, and I'll prove it," she said again. She was alone, surrounded. She needed someone on her side. Flinging open the door into the rest of the house, she shouted up the stairs. "Damon, come down here—I need you."

Footsteps hurried down the stairs.

"What's the matter?" Damon asked as he reached the hallway, rubbing sleep from his eyes. Negotiating with demons had made his life nocturnal, working at the hours that best suited his targets.

"Tell them that I can't be leader," Ines said as she led him into the kitchen. "That I can't take over from Shaw."

Leaning in the doorway, Damon looked around the room. His steady gaze was in sharp contrast to the eagerness with which the others looked at her, a hunger that verged on desperation in their eyes.

"Why don't you think you can do it?" he said at last.

"I..." Ines began, frustrated and bewildered. Of course she couldn't lead all these people. That was the whole point. "I don't know anything about it. I'd be terrible."

Damon shrugged. He didn't stand up straight to do it, creating a comedically lopsided gesture as one shoulder rose while the other stayed planted against the doorframe. It didn't quite make Ines laugh, but it eased some of the tension inside her, and she could tell by the smile at the corner of his mouth that he knew what he was doing.

"Think of the other leaders we've seen out there," he said. "Elizabeth Oldfield. The Archangel Michael. My oh-so-reasonable father. The ever-pompous voice of Field Marshal Sir Richard Brancepeth-Holmes, blaring at us out of royalist radio propaganda. Think about how they act, the things they do, the way they treat people. Do you really think that you would be a worse leader than any of them?"

"That doesn't mean I'll be good enough," Ines said uncertainly.

"It makes you better than our opponents," Damon said. "Especially as you're smart enough to listen to the clever people around you, unlike any of those evil windbags."

"I don't know," she said, staring down at her feet. She didn't feel like a leader right then. She felt as small as a mouse, surrounded by a world that could stamp it flat.

"It's okay to be afraid," Damon said. "I'm afraid to take command of demons, for fear of what I might do with that power.

You're afraid to muck this up. That's natural. But for the sake of everyone else, I think we both need to step up.

"I'll make you a deal. If you take charge of us, then I'll take on my responsibilities too. I'll do what it takes to rally demons to our cause, even if that's finally taking my place as Viscount Demi-Chron, over-titled spawn of Hell's finest. You give us direction, and I'll give us plenty of power to throw that way."

"You'll be good at that," she said, smiling from the heart outwards as she looked into his eyes.

"And so will you," he said.

Her smile widened at the confidence he was showing in her.

"All right." She looked around the room. Everyone was looking at her. Hema held a tray of tea and biscuits, ready to take them through to the next room.

"Are you ready, boss?" she asked.

"Give me five minutes," Ines said. "Then the rest of you can come in."

As she walked into the living room, the newly arrived mages looked up expectantly.

"My name is Ines Salgado," she said. "I'm the leader of the Earthly Host. I'm going to tell you what's happening with Tamsin Shaw. Then I'm going to explain how things work around here. After that, we'll all get down to saving the world."

CHAPTER 13
The Committee

"I can't believe this was sitting here unoccupied," Ines said as she watched the mages bringing the last supplies into the accommodation block. It wasn't a pretty building, being mostly the sort of concrete shell that was popular in the 1960s. Even the common room they were sitting in felt like the result of minimal effort, with sofas around the walls but little decoration or other furniture. But it had space for all of them, good views of anyone approaching, and room to work in. As bases went, they could do a lot worse.

"I can't believe I'm going to have my house to myself again," Marklew said.

"You'd be safer here with us," Ines said, her confidence turning to caution as she once again considered their exceptional luck. "Unless this is some sort of trap."

"How many times must I say it?" Marklew asked. "Renovations were meant to start a month ago, but then the Barrier broke, and everybody's priorities took a shift to the dramatic. That's why no one is here. Nothing to do with Elizabeth Oldfield."

"If you say so."

"You might still want someone to keep watch," Marklew said, looking towards the wooded hill behind the building and then the access road full of the mages' cars, its far end heading into town.

"Already done. It's almost like I can do this leadership business."

"Well then, I think I'll get going." Marklew smiled. "I plan to sprawl all over my living room, possibly naked."

"Ew!" Ines said, grimacing. The burly academic wasn't someone she wanted to think about in the nude. "Before you go, can I ask you something?"

"Of course. Shall we have a seat?"

Without waiting for an answer, Marklew walked over to the sofas in the far corner of the room and started on his planned sprawling. Joining him, Ines found herself taking up far less space, hunching over as she clutched her hands in her lap, fingers drumming restlessly against each other. She shifted one of her feet back and forth on the mottled brown carpet, watching the laces on her trainer bounce about.

"You don't seem terribly keen to talk," Marklew said.

"Sorry." Ines looked up at him. "I'm just not sure where to start."

"Is this about the boys?" Marklew asked.

"God, no!" Ines exclaimed, taken aback. "What makes you say that?"

"You've been living in my house," Marklew said. "I would have had to be a fool not to see what's going on. And besides, Tamsin told me about it. She was concerned about what might happen."

"Well, it's not that," Ines said. She was terribly aware of that other problem, but she didn't want to discuss it with

Marklew any more than she wanted to see him naked. "It's about me."

"Go on." He leaned forwards, a serious look on his face.

"Shaw thought that there was something special about me. Something that let me fight angels and demons when others couldn't."

"Indeed."

"We couldn't work out what it was. I want to know, but I'm not sure how to find out. Is there a way to better understand how magic works around me?"

Marklew sat back, stroking his beard as he stared thoughtfully into space.

"Off the top of my head, I'd say that your best option is to go to a place of power," he said. "If magic reacts differently to you, then something might happen there that provides a clue. Even if you don't understand it, we have a hall full of mages to help with interpretation.

"Even if that fails, it still might be a useful trip. People have been going to places of power for millennia in search of mystical guidance. Many visions and prophecies are now recognized as having come from magical forces acting on the subconscious, bringing insights that might otherwise never arise."

"Thank you," Ines said. "The next question is where—"

Yelling broke out in front of the building. Leaping to her feet, Ines looked out the window.

Half a dozen demons had appeared amid the parked cars, their bodies like those of unnaturally thin humans, spines protruding from all over their heads. They came vaulting across the vehicles in vast bounds, surrounding a pair of mages carrying boxes.

Drawing the knife she kept constantly up her sleeve, Ines ran out the door and towards the monsters. Two turned as she approached, and one launched a cloud of needle-fine spines in her direction.

Diving into a forward roll behind a van, Ines winced as her bruised shoulder hit the hard ground. The spines shot past where she had been, burying themselves in a wall.

The demons and mages clashed, magic flashing through the air, glowing weapons and spiny hands slashing at each other. Wriggling her way forward underneath the car, Ines approached a demon standing on the far side. She turned the last of her crawl into a lunge, cutting a deep wound in the back of the demon's leg. It swung around, screaming, as she sprang to her feet, the knife driving up towards its face.

With a sweep of its arm, the demon flung her back against the van. She landed hard, head spinning and the breath knocked from her lungs. The dark hole of the creature's mouth opened, its hands twisted, and a web of magic hurtled towards her.

With a bright flash, another spell hit the demon in the head. Its magic dissipated, its back arched, and then it ran screaming away up the hill.

Frustrated as she was at having been brought low, Ines forced a smile as she stood up and congratulated the mages on fending off the demons. She was a leader now, and she had to encourage people.

But, inside, she was twisted with disappointment. If she had learned what was special about her, then maybe she could have used it in the fight, and so avoided being almost knocked out. She needed to get a grip on this soon.

She needed to go to a place of power.

* * *

They had needed a name for the meetings of the main players in the Earthly Host, and Ines had settled on "the committee." Rumiel had wanted to call the group "the war council." Damon had suggested "the knitting circle" and then tried to tempt them into taking his joke seriously by saying it would confuse their enemies. "Executive," "cabinet," and "command group" had all been raised. But Ines liked "committee." It made the whole thing sound more democratic, and somehow less permanent, as if they were just coming together to plan an end-of-term party.

"First matter," Hema said, peering at the agenda she had scribbled on a scrap of paper. "Ines has something to discuss."

Half a dozen gazes turned to where she sat at the end of their improvised conference table. This space had once been a computer room—cables still sat in untidy piles in its corners, and the desks they had pushed together were full of holes for those wires to go through. But the table was mostly just a focal point, a way of setting the tone that business would be done. The state of its surface didn't really matter.

"I'm going out on my own tonight," Ines said. Murmurs of protest instantly rose from all and sundry. She raised her hand to silence them then continued. "Shaw thought that there was something special about me. She's not the only one. Whether I like it or not, I have to treat that seriously.

"If I have some sort of power, then I need to know what it is. It could provide a real edge in the struggle we're caught up in. There isn't time to mess about, running long, slow tests. I need to know as soon as I can.

"Mr. Marklew has helped me come up with a plan."

"Surely I'm Tim by now," Marklew said in mock indignation.

"Fine," Ines said, drumming her fingers on the table and trying to hide her impatience. This was serious business, and she was nervous enough about it without suffering interruptions and delays. "Tim has helped me to come up with a plan. I'm going to go to the cathedral, to a place there that's the richest in power of anywhere in Durham, and therefore anywhere in the north of England. He's suggested some ways I can release that power and see how it acts around me."

"You cannot do this alone," Rumiel said. "Our enemies are everywhere. They may attack you. I should be there to provide protection."

"No, I should," Damon said. "You draw too much attention, walking around glowing the whole time. I can provide the backup Ines needs without calling down trouble."

"You?" Rumiel glared at Damon. "A demon in the house of the Lord? This will disrupt all that Ines seeks to achieve. You must stay away."

"Of course, it's all about piety." Damon smirked. There was bitterness in the expression. "And not at all about trying to get her on her own. Thinking of making a move, are you?"

"Why should I not? We have—"

"Enough!" Ines banged her fist on the table. "Neither of you is coming with me. No one is."

"That doesn't sound safe," Hema said quietly.

"Maybe not, but it will be the most effective." Ines waved at Marklew. "You explain."

"Everyone in our little club touches upon magic," Marklew said. "Mages, angels, demons. Their presence could influence the flow of power, affecting what Ines experiences. That could give us false information. Our best hope is if she goes in there alone."

They sat in silence for a long moment. Ines could almost see the others considering objections and alternatives.

"You've only just taken over as leader," Damon said, first to reach the key point. "You're needed here."

"That's why we're having this meeting first," Ines said. "I want to put everything in order, so that the Host can work without me for the next week. That way, if something goes wrong, then you'll have time to pick a new leader.

"We'll put people in charge of different areas—defense, supplies, information gathering, research on the Barrier, anything else that seems important. We'll list their responsibilities. We'll decide how many of our people will work for each of them. We've got all afternoon to work it out, but if we do that, then we're in a better position even if I come straight back, safe and full of power."

"*When* you come straight back like that," Rumiel said, smiling confidently. "I believe in you."

"We all do," Damon said hurriedly, shooting Rumiel a toxic glare.

This was the other reason why Ines wanted to get away. It would give her time to muster her thoughts about these two. To sift through her feelings and try to work out what she wanted. It was impossible to do that with everybody calling upon her to make decisions and issue orders, but it needed to be done. As Shaw had said, there was too much at stake to let that situation fester.

Not for the first time, Ines desperately wished that her friend was with them instead of in the hospital, her battered body fighting for health and life. In her absence, the best that Ines could achieve was to do her proud.

"Hema has everything important listed on the agenda," she said. "Let's get on with this. I have somewhere I need to be at dusk."

CHAPTER 14
The Shrine of St. Cuthbert

As she approached the cathedral, Ines felt lighter than she had in days. The decision to come here hadn't been forced upon her by circumstances, as had happened with leading the Earthly Host. It hadn't come out of the demands of others. It wasn't even about others, not directly. It was her choice, the opportunity to learn more about herself, to work out who she was and who she wanted to be.

As she walked along a narrow street, its shops and restaurants closed, several windows boarded up, she thought about Damon and Rumiel. If she had only met one of them, then everything would be fine.

Thinking about either boy made her smile. Memories of kissing them stirred thoughts and imaginings she could never admit to her parents. The bond she had with Damon was like friendship reinforced a hundred times over. Just looking at Rumiel made her heart burst with excitement. How could she choose between those feelings?

The last time she had been near Palace Green, Hema and Jason had rescued her from Oldfield's mages. Happiness was replaced with barbed anger that hooked at her insides as she remembered Jason at that first encounter, and then days later, when Oldfield had killed him.

The woman had to be stopped. If only for that reason, what happened this evening was important.

The sun was starting to set as she came out onto the green. The cathedral loomed in front of her. It was still an amazing sight, now crowned with something stranger. Angels and demons flocked around it, dark and light shapes hovering in the air like moths drawn to a flame. The air grew hazy as they swirled around the building, not coming close enough to touch or to enter, just seeming to bask in its presence.

Any doubts she had about the power of the place evaporated at the sight.

No one else was to be seen anywhere on Palace Green. The demons and angels might not be fighting each other, but they would still make dangerous company for any mages. Even ordinary people would have trouble not seeing all these supernatural beings, the mind's trick of blanking them out failing in the face of so many. It was no wonder that people were staying away instead of seeking the comfort of the church.

Still, she approached cautiously, so as to avoid drawing the attention of either angels or demons. She didn't want to risk any interruption. According to Marklew, this was a powerful time of day, and she wanted to make the most of it.

Whoever had left the cathedral last had left the door wide open, possibly distracted by the chaos of the world, possibly hoping to provide sanctuary in these troubled times. Despite her fears, none of the angels or demons even glanced in Ines's direction as she walked through the door and into the cold interior.

The inside of the cathedral was every bit as stunning as the outside. Stone pillars the size of giant redwoods held up a vast vaulted ceiling. Intricate decoration on sturdy construction paid homage to the strength and complexity of God. Ines's footsteps echoed back to her as she passed rows of empty seats, tombs of medieval nobles, and a plaque memorializing miners lost in the depths of the earth. Like any church, it was a memorial to loss as well as to life, all the more so without a congregation.

She bypassed the pulpit and choir stalls that provided a focus for services, heading for a place singled out by Marklew. Up a short flight of stone steps, she entered something like a raised room within the cathedral proper. Above it hung a brightly painted image of a saint in blue-and-red robes, hands spread wide, his body framed by a golden sunburst. In the middle of the floor was a slab of dark-grey stone as large as a door, the word CUTHBERTUS engraved upon it.

This was the shrine of St. Cuthbert.

Marklew had told her a little about the ancient saint and the miracles surrounding his body, which was said to have remained perfectly preserved hundreds of years after his death. He was a symbol of faith across the region, this shrine a place of miracles and deep, desperate prayer.

The power was so strong that even Ines could see it. A haze filled the air between the slab of cold, dead stone on the floor and the bright, life-filled painting hanging above it. It was as if someone had trapped a whole summer's worth of heat haze and focused it in that one spot. The blurring of the air outside the cathedral was nothing by comparison.

Ines swallowed. Now that she was here, she felt nervous. But she had come this far, and there could be no excuses. Folding her legs beneath her, she sat in front of that haze, closed her eyes, emptied her mind, and let the world in.

Nothing happened. She tried meditating as Marklew had taught her, taking deep breaths and letting go of any thoughts that intruded. But no vision came, no insight emerged from her subconscious.

She opened her eyes and held her hand out near that column of power in the center of the room. Her fingers tingled as they came close, but there was no sign that her presence had any effect on the magic. It didn't waver, didn't fade, didn't shift or swirl or flow into her. She might as well not have been there.

Marklew had told her to be patient, and she tried. For an hour, she sat there, as dusk turned into night outside the cathedral. She prayed. She thought. She meditated. She got up and strode impatiently back and forth.

Nothing.

She stared at the magic-filled air in front of her. There was one thing she could try. It was terrifying, but what other options were there? She couldn't wait forever. Her friends needed her.

As boldly as she could, she stepped into the column of power.

The tingling she had felt in her fingers now filled every part of her body. It grew in intensity, like an itch that could not be scratched. Her arms and legs shook, and her chest convulsed, her breath becoming broken. Her eyes burned, and fire blazed in her mind.

Tears streamed down her face. Her whole world had become pain.

She could still see the power all around her and feel it coursing through her. It tugged her in every direction, stretching her out like a victim on a medieval rack. Her muscles strained and joints groaned as the magic started to tear her apart.

With certainty greater than love or faith or anything in the world, she knew that she was going to die.

Then she felt it. A single small place of stillness at the front of her belly. She dragged her hand around, muscles straining, flesh feeling as if it were being flayed. With trembling fingers, she reached into the pocket of her hoodie. The pain eased from her hand as it closed around the scrap of cloth her father had given her—the protective charm.

Drawing it from her pocket, she brought it up in front of her eyes. The symbol soothed her, a sign of love and a thing of magic. The air grew still around it—just a small spot in this inferno of power, but a beginning. Pressing it against her heart, she found the strength at last to take a step forward, and then another, pushing herself out of the pillar of pain.

She stumbled clear and collapsed onto the cool stones, clutching the cloth to her.

* * *

A memory of pain lingered throughout Ines's body. Every part of her ached. Everything she touched seemed to hit her with the force of a punch, and she was amazed to see that her skin was not all bruised.

As she walked back through the streets, she took deep breaths again, stilling the trembling of her body, trying to muster her thoughts.

She had failed. All that pain and patience had been for nothing. No vision, no insight, nothing but agony and its aftermath. She was a fool. What would the others say when they heard how close she had brought herself to death? They would close in around her tighter than ever. Those protective instincts she had faced in the committee would become a hundred times worse. She couldn't face that.

So, instead, she would face her frustration alone. She could tell them that she had failed—that much was true. She could even tell them about the useless waiting for a vision. But her final act, and the terror she had been through, that was for her alone.

In her pocket, her grip tightened around the protective ward. She would never be able to thank her father enough for what he had given her.

Bustle and noise filled the space outside the Earthly Host's headquarters. Rumiel, Helda, and an angel Ines didn't recognize were flying in circles low above the parked cars. Damon was caught in intense conversation with a pair of gargoyle-like demons. Mages stood in groups, practising spells and magical shields.

"What's happening?" Ines asked as she reached Damon.

"Your mother," he said with a sudden smile. He pointed up. "That new angel arrived at dusk. Word's getting around about the work Rumiel and Helda have been doing, helping people who are in trouble because of the war. He decided that was what the angels should be doing, so came to join them."

"What does that have to do with my mum?" Ines asked, excitement battling pain for her attention.

"He knows where she's being held. Saw mages in grey suits taking a woman there and setting up security wards. Oldfield was one of them. The woman fits your mum's description."

He put his hands on her shoulders, staring intently into her eyes. Ines suppressed the urge to wince at the touch on tender flesh.

"Ines, this is it!" Damon said. "We can rescue her at last."

"Good," Ines said. "Let's do it."

"I thought you'd be more excited," Damon said, looking concerned.

"Let's do it now." Ines forced a grin. "Is that better?"

"It'll do." Damon laughed. "But don't you want to wait a bit so that we can plan and prepare?"

"No." Ines had had enough of waiting. Right now, she felt as if her whole existence had been made up of waiting and of pain. She couldn't wait anymore.

"No, we act now. We can't risk them moving her."

More than that, if Oldfield was there, then she didn't want to risk the minister getting away. She had kidnapped Ines's parents, endangered her brother, nearly killed her friend. Ines couldn't do anything about the force that had caused her such agony today, but she could do something about Oldfield.

She could kill her.

CHAPTER 15
Amateur Moves

"It's not what I expected." Ines looked down the hill towards a large country pub, its facade illuminated by the soft light of early morning. The tables out front were empty, the doors closed. Occasional glimpses of movement between the half-drawn curtains were the only sign of life.

"What's the plan, boss?" Hema asked.

It took Ines a moment to realize that the question was directed at her. Crouched behind the low wall hiding them from any sentries at the pub, she considered her options.

"Could we get anybody around there to the left?" She popped her head up and pointed to a shady patch of trees beyond the pub's parking lot. "Without being seen, I mean."

"I could," Damon said. "If I just take demons, it'll be easier."

"Okay." Ines glanced at the two creatures who had started following Damon around. A few months ago, she would have been intimidated by them, with their twitching tails, pointed teeth, and glowing red eyes set into dark-grey skin. Now, all she saw were two under-sized and underpowered little demons, whom she could only hope had something of power to offer in a fight.

Peering over the wall, she looked again at the open fields and roads surrounding the pub and the many windows crowding its three floors. Once they hit that open space, they would be sitting ducks for magical attacks.

"Damon, get around that side as quick as you can," she said. "Rumiel, you and Helda fly high enough that they're unlikely to see you. Hover above the roof and wait for us to make our move."

"As you command." Both angels bowed, wings burst from their backs, and they soared towards the heavens.

"The rest of you, prepare defensive magics," Ines said, looking around at the dozen black-clad mages. "If you can, make use of your specialties—that way our defenses should be more powerful than any crude Ministry-style attacks they throw."

The mages nodded and began their rituals. Some focused on their hands, moving them in sweeping patterns. Others muttered incantations. Two moved their whole bodies in flowing movements like tai chi, one raising rocks into the air as she did so, the other bending his limbs like rubber.

Five minutes passed while their supernatural allies got into position and the mages prepared for battle.

"This is it," Ines said as she caught a glimpse of movement in the trees. "Remember, we've got two aims—rescue my mum and take down Oldfield. Any questions?"

They shook their heads.

"Good. Let's go."

They followed the line of walls down the hill until there was no more cover to be had. Then Ines leapt into a sprint, rushing towards the pub.

A couple of the mages were able to keep up with her. She was grateful for the magical haze they created in the air, especially once shouts and bolts of magic started hurtling towards them. There was a flash as an attack was absorbed by their defenses, and another as a bolt of power hit the road to their left.

Just as Damon had predicted, demons began to appear in the nearby fields, drawn by the scent of human aggression like sharks closing in on blood in the water. It was the third purpose of this attack, the one the mages didn't need to think about—impressing some demons so that Damon could drag them into his service. Recruitment for their cause.

The breath rasped in Ines's lungs as they approached the pub. Her joints ached, the remnants of her pain at the shrine coming back stronger. She had thrown caution to the wind in her eagerness to use the element of surprise. She needed to be careful not to exhaust herself, even as she pushed for victory.

The sound of an engine was followed by the screech of tires. A car shot out from behind the pub. The sleek form of a red BMW swept away from them, a grey-clad mage behind the wheel. In the passenger seat, unmistakable in her dark pinstripe suit and tightly controlled blond hair, was Elizabeth Oldfield.

Ines slowed, glancing between the pub and the car. Should she let Oldfield get away and focus on rescuing her mother? Or should they go after the car, relying on the fact that the prisoner would still be here when they got back? Should she try to deal with both?

"What now?" Hema asked, appearing at Ines's shoulder.

In front of them, a black-clad mage waved his hands. Fresh shoots and leaves burst forth from a wooden picnic table, the planks rediscovering their origins as trees, the foliage rising to hide the mages from their enemies, now less than a hundred yards away.

"That bitch is going to get away," Ines growled, hate for Oldfield boiling up inside her. If looks could have killed, then the BMW would have exploded. She ground her teeth in frustration. "Damn it, we have to stay focused. Keep going for the pub. I'll rip Oldfield a new hole later."

The mages looked at her, taken aback.

"Go on!" Ines snapped, pointing towards the pub. Rumiel and Helda hovered at upper windows, trying to fight their way in, and she could hear shouts from around the back. There was no time to waste.

The mages began their advance again. But the looks they had given her made Ines pause for a moment, remembering her words and the hatred that had driven them out of her. She found herself unsettled by the realization that those words really had been her own, that she was capable of such malice, even towards someone as awful as Oldfield.

Reaching into her pocket, she closed her fingers around her father's ward, the familiar little piece of cloth bringing her back to herself.

She had work to do.

The Ministry mages were putting up a fierce fight. To the left, a window had melted from the heat emanating from magics clashing around it. To the right, another window had been smashed in, and a melee had broken out across its jagged remains, the rubber-like mage whipping his arms back and forth against defenders with glowing clubs and shields. The front door trembled, green shoots springing from its wood then withering away as spell and counter-spell hit.

"There's more than one way to beat magic," she said.

There was a trash can by the door, a round plastic one with a metal interior. She wrenched off the top and pulled out the metal part, tipping old garbage down herself and across the ground. Swinging the improvised battering ram, she slammed it into the straining door. Splinters flew from the writhing, twisting, magic-filled wood. Another swing, and the lock creaked but didn't break, though jagged points of wood protruded around it. She made the third swing with her whole body, bruised flesh filling with pain as her shoulder hit.

The wood around the lock disintegrated, and the door burst open.

Stumbling into the darkened interior of the building, Ines saw a glowing weapon swinging towards her. She ducked, rolled, and rose to her feet with a knife in her hand, facing a dozen grimly determined Ministry mages, their magical clubs and shields raised.

"Ines!" Hema yelled behind her. "Ines, get back out here!"

Muttering darkly, Ines backed up through the doorway. Two of the mages stepped forwards, filling the gap. Now it would be twice as hard to get past them.

"What is it?" she snapped as she turned towards her ally.

"Oldfield's back." Hema pointed up the road.

Two hundred yards away, cars were screeching to a halt, blocking the road as their occupants clambered out. Dozens of men and women in grey suits, hands glowing with power. Behind them stood Elizabeth Oldfield, sunlight gleaming off the golden pin in her lapel.

"Did you really think it would be that easy?" Oldfield called out. "That I would flee from your pitiful little band?"

"I'm going to kill you!" Ines screamed, anger and pain making her voice fierce. "By the time we're done, you'll be nothing but a bloodstained memory."

Oldfield tipped her head back and laughed.

"Enough nonsense." The minister waved her troops forwards. "Destroy them."

Across the fields, the demons crept closer, licking their lips and cackling at the sight of war. Beetle-men and giant slugs, tiny gargoyles and loose-limbed figures like scarecrows made of razor-blades, all began to close in, grinning as they tasted the hate.

Rumiel and Helda swept down, concrete crumpling at the force of their landings, he wielding a blazing sword, she a battle-axe with an icy silver glow. Even with them at their side, Ines's rebel mages were badly outnumbered by the Ministry.

"Demons!" Damon shouted, appearing around the corner of the building. He raised his hands like an orator facing his audience. "In the name of my father, great Chron, Lord of the Third Circle, I command you. Raise arms and defend my friends."

A halo of darkness appeared around his head. His eyes became black, unblinking pits in which currents of something deeper stirred.

A murmur ran through the demons. A few bent at the knee.

"You are not Chron," a slouching figure screeched. "I have beheld Chron. He is muscle and horn, malice and menace. Only he can claim his name."

"Pretender!" another demon yelled.

"Amateur!" bellowed a thing like a vast slug.

"Loser!" shouted a pair of tiny imps.

The magic held around Damon's head, but the darkness died in his eyes. His expression fell through disappointment into a bitter, shut-down anger as the creatures cackled at him.

The air tingled as Oldfield's mages, emboldened by Damon's failure, went back onto the attack. A mage slumped to the ground as a spell hit him, and Helda grimaced as razor shards of power sliced through her shoulder.

Ines looked at the pub doorway. Somewhere behind there was her mother, still victim to the whims of Elizabeth Oldfield. She wanted to fling herself at the mages blocking the way, to fight through them, smash open every door that stood before her, and let the prisoner free. She wanted to make her mother proud.

But the Ministry mages were advancing down the road, their attacks emerging from behind a solid wall of magical shields. There was no way her outnumbered force could stand against them.

"Retreat," she called out, something inside her dying at the word. It had been a strand of hope holding her up since she returned from the cathedral, that had helped her to cope with the pain and terror of the shrine. The thought that her mother could now be freed. It made her feel small and uncertain to let it go, but she had other people to care for now. All the mages, angels, and demons who had sided with her. All these people who had put their safety in her care.

Rumiel and Helda each grabbed a pair of weak or injured mages, taking one under each arm, and swept up into the sky. Damon slammed his fist against the wall, blood seeping from his knuckles for a moment before he took hold of time, vanishing with his demons and a few more of the mages.

The rest backed up, shields raised and retreating up the road.

"Come on." Hema grabbed Ines, dragging her towards a gate to the side of the pub. Magic swirled as she twisted her hand.

"What about the others?" Ines looked back at the few mages still making a fighting retreat.

"You're too important to risk," Hema said.

They stepped through the gateway, and the whole world changed.

CHAPTER 16
Picking Up the Pieces

It looked to Ines as if she were standing in a dark corridor, except that there were no walls, no ceiling, just the void of space. The walls were like a night sky in the depths of winter, black and littered with the gleaming points of stars. Her breath frosted in front of her face.

Stretching out in front of her was a line of doors and gateways. Some were modern, the front doors of houses. Others were the ancient wood of churches, the glass panels of office buildings, or the rusted iron of abandoned factories. Many were nothing more than pairs of posts or rickety wooden gates from farmers' fields.

"Quickly," Hema gasped, fingers tightening on Ines's upper arm. Ice spread across the mage's face as she headed towards one of the nearest gates, pushed it open, and hurled them both through.

They emerged into a grassy field littered with cow pats. Several cows looked up at them as they appeared, then looked away, entirely disinterested. Ines stumbled but kept her feet, while Hema tumbled to the ground next to her. The earth frosted in a ring around the mage, even as ice crystals in her hair began to thaw.

"Are you all right?" Ines asked as she crouched beside Hema. She pulled off her hoodie and spread it across the other woman, trying to warm her up.

"Need a few minutes," Hema said. "Moving from gate to gate is harder than stepping out of the one I came in by. Taking someone else makes it a thousand times worse."

"Why the ice?" Ines asked.

"All magic has a price," Hema said.

"Blood and pain for demons," Ines said, pieces clicking into place. "And warmth for you?"

"Smart." Hema stood. The ice was gone from her face, but her lips were still blue. "That's why you're leader."

Their field was on a hilltop. In the valley below, Ines saw the pub they had just come from. The fighting was over, tiny grey-clad figures regrouping in the road. Nothing good could come from staying so close.

Hema had a good sense of direction, but that didn't make the journey back to Durham easy. Trudging through fields and woods, ducking through back gardens, and wading through streams, they tried to avoid main roads in case Oldfield's people were hunting stragglers.

Several times, they hid behind walls or buildings as patrols of armed soldiers marched past. Random travelers would draw suspicious attention in what was clearly now a warzone, and that wasn't something they wanted.

Every village they passed through showed signs of the war. Cratered roads. Shattered shells of buildings. Bullet-riddled walls. The burnt-out remains of three tanks at a crossroads. They were lucky to go ten minutes without hearing gunfire somewhere nearby.

As they were coming into town, a pair of jets shot through the air, low enough to rattle windows. The one in front was trailing smoke, the other pursuing it with guns blazing.

"We need to regroup," Ines said, as much to distract herself from the destruction as to prepare herself for their return to base. "Work out our next move."

"Whatever you need," Hema said, "I've got your back."

* * *

A dozen of the Earthly Host's finest sat around the improvised council table in the old computer room. At the end of the table, Ines drummed her fingers and fought to stifle a scream of rage. Once again, the war council was descending into recrimination.

"The ambush was too well laid," Rumiel said. "Someone must have told them that we were coming."

"Yes!" an imp said, pointing its talon in a series of sharp stabs towards Hema and the mages. "One of them tells its friends, yes?"

"That's ridiculous," Hema said. "We suffered as much as anyone."

"Mages are tricksy," the imp said. "Always trapping and deceiving those of other worlds."

"We deceive?" Hema said. "You're demons. You work for the prince of lies."

"But never for Oldfield. No old loyalties there, yes?"

"No loyalties at all," the angel Helda said. "I saw you not in the battle—was this all just some scheme to bring destruction upon us?"

She glared at the imp, her eyes burning with hatred. It responded with a snarl and a raised finger.

"I give this for your destruction!" it hissed.

"Well, that's about as helpful as you were in the fight," Hema said.

"The imps helped," Damon said. "Their powers might not be as flashy as yours or that of the angels, but we were doing our part before things went wrong."

"Demons always do their part," Rumiel said, narrowing his eyes. "But it is always the part of evil."

"As opposed to righteous slaughter?" Damon stood, glaring across the table.

"Don't go telling me now about the evil of demons and the virtue of angels. I've been hunted by your kind, seen them almost kill Ines, and I will not have my followers talked to like this."

Rumiel rose to respond, while Hema raised her voice to be heard. Suddenly, they were all shouting, the room full of angry words and furious faces as everyone tried to blame everyone else.

"Enough!" Ines yelled at the top of her lungs. She banged her fist down so hard that the whole table bounced an inch into the air.

Silence fell.

"Sit down, all of you," she said, glaring at them.

Behind the mask of her fury, she felt like a mouse trying to intimidate an elephant. Everyone here had magical power except for her. Any of them could flatten her in a fight if that power was unleashed. And now they were looking expectantly at her.

She couldn't let them talk about what had happened—that just led to recriminations. She couldn't get them discussing the next step together, because everyone had a different agenda, and the minute they disagreed, the blame started flying again.

If she wanted to hold their alliance together, she needed to give them a goal. She needed an enemy for them to fight.

"We got overambitious going after Oldfield," she said, terribly aware of her own part in that plan. "We need an enemy that we can pick off more easily, and Helda has given us one."

"I have?" The angel looked at her in surprise.

"You said Sanctus was living at that church by the marketplace, right?"

"Verily, he and two others."

"Good. Up until now, the Blazing Host have come after us, but we've never taken the fight to them. Tonight, that changes. Tonight, we take one of their biggest bastards down."

* * *

The Church of St. Nicholas was a traditional Church of England building at the end of the market square. Right in the center of town, it wasn't a place they could attack in large numbers, not if they wanted to avoid drawing attention. That was fine with Ines. Many on their side needed time to recover, even if they wouldn't admit it. A precision assault gave her an excuse to leave people behind.

Githtor and Werrenmak, two of Damon's imps, flanked Ines as she strode across the marketplace towards the church.

"Don't like this, no," Githtor lisped, twitching her tail back and forth in agitation. Neither imp was more than four feet tall, and they might almost have been taken for frightened children as they stared agitatedly at the house of God.

"Not fun," Werrenmak agreed. "Not fun, not fun, not fun."

"You get to fight an angel," Ines said. "Won't you enjoy that?"

"Like that, yes," Githtor said, flapping into the air on tiny, bat-like wings.

"Fun," Werrenmak agreed, cracking the knuckles of his feet as well as his hands.

Three tongues shot out from Githtor's mouth. They slammed into the church door, and it slammed back on its hinges, hitting the wall with a heavy thud.

"Subtle," Werrenmak cackled.

"Perfect," Ines said as she strode through the door, a knife in her hand.

An angel stalked towards them. His glowing white clothes were shaped like those of a Victorian gentleman, from the pointed tips of his shoes to the peak of his top hat. He drew a sword-stick from his ivory cane, the blade bursting into flames as it touched the air.

His smug expression turned to shock as Githtor's tongues shot out again, entangling his sword hand. As he tried to shake them off, Werrenmak scampered past and crouched down behind him. Distracted by the demons, he barely even reacted as Ines ran towards him, slamming into his chest with her good shoulder. The angel stepped back, tripped over Werrenmak, and crashed to the ground.

Another angel rushed towards them between the rows of seats lining the nave. Githtor shot out her tongues once more, but the angel ducked just as Hema appeared out of the air in an archway behind it. The tongues hit her in the face, and she staggered back, while the angel kept coming.

Glass shattered, and Rumiel swept in through the remains of a window. He swung his flaming sword at the angel, forcing him to back off.

"Get out of the way!" he yelled at Werrenmak as the imp scurried around behind the angel.

"Helping!" Werrenmak squawked. "Helping, helping, helping!"

Spinning around, the angel kicked Werrenmak, sending him crashing back through rows of seats.

Meanwhile, Ines was grappling with the first angel on the ground. The two of them rolled over and over on the cold stone slabs, she trying to bring her knife to bear, he trying to twist his sword into her.

"Someone help!" she shouted.

"Gladly." Sanctus dropped from the ceiling, flagstones shattering beneath him as he landed. With his broad shoulders and white tracksuit, he could have been a boxer or just another townie heading down to the pub. He raised his fist, brass knuckles gleaming as he prepared to swing them down into her face.

Ines fought back her panic. This wasn't perfect, but they hadn't expected perfect. What mattered was what she did now.

As long as she could survive the next two seconds.

The fist swept down.

Ines twisted, bringing the other angel around where she had been.

Sanctus's fist hit his comrade's face in an explosion of light. As the Victorian angel shuddered in pain, Ines slammed her knife in where a human's ribs would have been. The creature screamed and curled in on himself. He would live, but he would play no further part in this fight.

Sanctus swung a kick at Ines. She just managed to roll clear, shouting for Werrenmak as she did. Sanctus raised his foot again, ready to stamp down on her.

Werrenmak shot across the floor, rolling like a tiny boulder. He slammed into Sanctus's leg, knocking it out from under him. As the angel crashed to the ground, Werrenmak flipped over and landed on his face, battering at the glowing features with a flurry of small punches and kicks.

Rumiel and the other angel were fighting up and down the nave. Both had swords drawn. They slashed, stabbed, and parried, the flames of their blades charring furniture and flagstones as blows were dodged or knocked aside. It was like watching an old swashbuckling movie, two expert fencers dancing back and forth, their blades an extension of their bodies. It was beautiful to watch but getting them nowhere.

"Rumiel, to Hema," Ines called out.

Rumiel dropped his sword. As his opponent swung at him, he ducked and lunged forward. The blow scraped down his back in a gout of flames, but he ignored it. Grabbing the other angel by the front of his coat, he swung him around and flung him to the doorway in which Hema stood.

The mage spread her arms wide. As the angel hit, the two of them vanished. A moment later, she reappeared, frost-covered and grinning.

"He won't be back for a while," she said.

By now, Sanctus had gained the upper hand against Werrenmak, pinning the demon to the ground, holding him at arm's length while he punched him over and over again. Githtor screamed as she clung to the angel's back, tongues wrapped around his throat, but he showed no signs of slowing.

Ines got to her feet. Grabbing a piece of a broken chair, she swung it at the angel's head.

He caught it before it even got close.

"Nice try, human," he sneered, "but you're not strong enough to take me out."

"No, I'm not," Ines agreed. "But he is."

Sanctus looked up just as Rumiel's foot hit him in the face. The kick sent him flying, seats shattering as he plowed through them. At last, he hit a pillar and slid unconscious to the ground.

It was the most satisfying thing Ines had seen all week.

"What now?" Hema asked.

"Now you find a nice secure door to lock him up behind," Ines said. "After that, we finally get to celebrate a victory."

CHAPTER 17
Hunter in the Night

It was amazing the difference a single success could make.

Within an hour of their returning to base, word got around to everyone. The mages gathered in the common room, grinning and chattering excitedly. They congratulated Hema and Ines. Some cautiously approached Rumiel, offering their appreciation for his part. A few even talked to the imps, though between the uncertainty of the humans and the imps' own tendency to mock, punch, and pinch them, those conversations seldom lasted.

Then the other angels appeared—four now, including Helda—and gathered around Rumiel, their expressions serious as he explained what had happened to Sanctus and the others. After all, these had been their comrades until just days before. Like the mages before them, they were struggling to come to terms with their growing civil war.

The demons coped far more easily. Soon, a couple dozen were clustered in a corner of the room, most of them unfamiliar to Ines. Most were small demons—imps and doglike creatures. But there were others as well—beasts of shadows, spines, and sinister eyes.

"This is the best thing that's ever happened for demon recruitment," Damon said, appearing beside Ines in a corner of the room. "They've so seldom had a chance to fight the angels directly, never mind to beat one. Githtor and Werrenmak are becoming folk heroes."

"It's such a relief having something good to talk about," Ines said.

"And it's all thanks to you." Damon discreetly squeezed her hand then let go to grab a donut from a box being passed around. Someone had gone out for celebratory snacks, leaving packets and boxes of junk food scattered around the room. Some of the mages were even opening bottles of beer.

"We'll have to make sure most people stay sober," Ines said. "After this, the angels could come for us at any time."

"That was always true," Damon said. "But you're right. We should maybe get the committee together this evening as well, talk about our next move."

Ines shook her head. "No need for a formal meeting yet. Everyone's having too much fun."

"No formal meeting, huh?" Damon looked sidelong at her. "But you're still going to talk about it with people?"

It seemed unavoidable. Everyone who mattered was in the room, and she couldn't help noticing the way they looked at her from time to time. Celebrating but expectant, wanting to know where their leader would take them next. They probably all had ideas of their own— Damon's subtle and cautious, Rumiel's headstrong and bold, Hema's calculating but concerned for those around her. If she could have relaxed enough to really enjoy the party, Ines might have ignored all that. But their future was on her mind as well, and she had her own priorities. Her mother. The boys. Oldfield.

A group of mages with beers in their hands, Hema among them, ambled over with mischievous grins on their faces.

"We know you won't let us call you 'Minister,'" one of them said, "so we came up with an alternative."

From behind his back, he pulled a crown made out of the cardboard from a box of beer, decorated with bottle tops for gems. The words "QUEEN INES" had been scrawled across the front in marker pen.

"Your majesty," the mages intoned in mock seriousness, bowing before her.

All around, people laughed at their antics. Ines shifted uncomfortably, her cheeks glowing hot. She'd never been comfortable with this sort of humor, or with being the center of a public display. She wanted to just quietly slip away into a corner, but Hema flashed her an urgent look, flicking her eyes towards the crown to signal the need to take it. Being leader meant being part of the fun, like it or not.

"Thank you." Ines took the crown and placed it on her head. She forced a smile as she struggled for something to say. "I shall wear it with pride."

This seemed to be enough. There were cheers, a giggle-riddled shout of "God save the queen!" and then the jovial royalists dispersed.

Hema lingered, smiling at Ines and her crown.

"I almost tried to talk them out of it," she said. "Now I see how daft you look, I'm glad I didn't."

"Thanks," Ines said, fighting the urge to remove the crown.

"So what next?" Hema asked, her expression turning serious. "I mean after this evening."

Ines relaxed. Any subject was better than going back to jokes about being queen.

"We need to tackle Oldfield," she said. "As long as she's around, the Ministry remain strong and coordinated. So we shift our focus onto taking her out."

"I'm not sure we need to do that," Hema said. "The more time passes, the more mages are coming over to our side. Soon, she won't have a support base at all."

"Not soon enough," Ines said. "If she hits us hard during that time, then she could do huge damage. Will people keep coming to our side then?"

"So we plan to defend ourselves," Damon said.

"And wait while the world descends further into chaos?" Ines snapped. "No, we need to be able to act without her interfering. We need to take her out."

"What do you mean by 'take her out'?" Damon asked, his handsome brow furrowing.

"Whatever it takes," Ines said.

A look of concern passed between Damon and Hema. Ines tensed, ready for an even more uncomfortable conversation.

"My Ines!" Rumiel swept in between the others, grabbed her around the waist, and lifted her into the air. "Hero of all!"

As he lowered her, their faces came close together. A thrill ran through Ines at having him so close, at the thought that he might get carried away in his excitement and kiss her. But there was fear of that too, with Damon so close.

Strong as Rumiel's grip was, it couldn't stop her wriggling free.

"I need to get some fresh air," she announced. "I'll see you all later."

As fast as she could go without breaking into a run, she headed for the door.

* * *

Ines shivered and clutched her arms around her knees, pulling herself in tight to preserve what heat she had. It was cold and dark on the moonlit hillside, and she had been in too much of a rush to think of bringing a coat. That had been fine as she cycled out of Durham, burning off nervous energy as she propelled the bike along darkened roads, but now she was regretting her haste.

The pub at the bottom of the hill looked invitingly warm. Oldfield's mages had set up lights around the perimeter, some electric and some magical, so that they could see attackers coming. There was even a bonfire blazing around the back, though Ines didn't know if that was mostly for light or for magical ritual purposes. Its orange glow reminded her of Guy Fawkes nights when she was younger, watching the bonfire blaze while she waited for the fireworks to be lit, standing with Toby between Mum and Dad.

The cozy nostalgia was followed by her all-too-familiar rage. The woman who had taken that from her was somewhere in that pub. If she could find a way in, or if Oldfield were to wander out on her own, then Ines could end this. She could make the world into a better, safer place.

Within the shelter of her hoodie, fingers tightened around the handle of her knife. Black shapes shifted closer in the darkness, wild demons savoring the taste of her hate.

Let them. Let that rage burn the whole world if it meant the fall of Elizabeth Oldfield.

"Ines." A soft voice came from behind her.

Whirling around, she pulled the knife from her sleeve and crouched, ready for combat.

A familiar slim silhouette stood on the brow of the hill.

"Here," Damon said, holding something out towards her. "I brought you a coat."

"How did you find me?" she asked, turning back to her surveillance of the pub.

"Like I couldn't tell what was on your mind." Damon draped the coat around her shoulders then sat down beside her. "I don't think this is a healthy way to act, but if you're determined, then I'm here for you."

"Thank you."

Even without those words, Damon's voice would have reassured her. Some of her tension eased away, and she leaned against him, resting her head on his shoulder. Damon wrapped his arm around her, and they sat like that for a while, Ines enjoying the warmth of friendship and of body heat on a cold, bitter night.

"Am I losing it?" she asked at last.

"No," Damon replied.

"Yes," said another voice behind them. "If it is your life, then the answer is most definitely yes."

Light suddenly filled the field around them, its brightness blinding Ines. She leapt to her feet, blinking and drawing her knife. As her vision returned, she saw half a dozen angels closing in on them. They were dressed in long white robes, hair tied back behind their heads, wings spread wide behind them. In their hands, they held flaming swords, swinging them in wide, intimidating arcs that left no space for escape. In any other moment, the sight would have been stunning, their strength, beauty, and brightness making a breathtakingly glorious vision. Here and now, they struck terror into Ines's heart.

Damon held out his pocket watch, hands shifting as he pulled in power. The air wavered between him and the nearest angel as he cast his spell.

The angel's movements slowed, his sword swinging almost to a halt as time slowed down for him. But then he grew faster again, walking towards them with his brothers and sisters in arms, encircling them in an ever-tightening wall of muscle and flame.

"Pitiful demon-spawn," the angel said, laughing. "You think you have the power to hold me?"

"He will now." Ines slashed her blade across the back of her arm. It was a long, shallow cut that left a chunk of skin flapping, drawing much blood and pain without digging into muscle or bone. She gritted her teeth as the pain washed across her in a terrible wave.

"Ines!" Damon yelled in alarm.

"Use it!" she said. "Use the power."

She shook her arm, spattering him with blood. Immediately, the air surrounding his watch swirled with renewed magical force. For a moment, he hesitated, eyes filled with concern for her. But then determination took hold. Spinning around, he cast the magic across the angels. Each one froze as the spell hit, turning them into a circle of glowing statues.

Dropping her knife so that she could stem the flow of blood, Ines ran through the gap between two of the angels, heading down the hill.

"Are you mad?" Damon shouted as he ran after her. "You're heading straight for the mages."

"And so will the angels if they follow us," Ines said. "If we can turn them on each other, then—"

"No," a deep voice said in front of her.

The air blazed with light once more. Sliding to a halt, Ines fell on the dew-dampened grass. Squinting up into the light, she saw a dozen more angels standing over her. In the center was a figure in plate armor, a look of supreme arrogance on his face.

The archangel Michael.

CHAPTER 18
Meetings Between Leaders

Eyes bright and hard as diamonds drilled into Ines, until she thought that they must penetrate to her very soul.

"Ines Salgado," Michael said, raising his sword. "The hour of judgement is upon you." He looked past her, his angular face stiff with scorn. "And who is this?"

The light of the angels illuminated Damon's face as he stood over Ines. His eyes were black pits in his pale skin, deep and fathomless.

"In the world of men, I am Damon Lorus," he said. "But to you, star-spawn of a burning realm, I am the Demi-Chron, heir apparent to the Third Circle."

S.A. Beck

"I care not whose seed you come from, boy," Michael sneered. "I will slice you in two and think no more of it. Demon, man, or half-breed bastard, none shall stand who stand only as a child."

"You are right," Damon said. "And so I take my name."

He held his hands out in front of him, shoulder width apart. A black ball grew in the air between them, like the one with which he had once been given power. But this was larger, deeper, a rent in the fabric of reality.

"I am the Lord Crius," Damon said. "Divider of years. Watcher of stars. He who splits age and eon. I arrive upon the fall of an old order and herald the coming of the new."

As he pulled his hands apart, the darkness spread. It muted the light from the angels, turning what had seemed as bright as dawn into the muted grey of late dusk. Only Michael shone as brightly as he once had.

"My age has just begun, demon," Michael said. "My legions are many, and you are alone. Your new order shall fall stillborn upon this dirt."

"Your legions may be many, but my circle are ever-present," Damon said. "Spawn of the Third Circle, in my own name and by my own power I command you, to me!"

"I thought that you would never ask." Loose-limbed and gangling, the demon Eldervain, whom Ines had seen before only as Chron's messenger, stepped into the light. He still wore his broad-brimmed hat and loose suit, but the jacket was swept back, revealing a pair of guns like something out of a cowboy film, six-shooters as black and slippery as an oil slick.

All around, the demons who had watched from the darkness stepped forwards. Each in turned bowed its head to Damon then moved around to form a cordon between the angels and their targets.

Michael's eyes darted to the left and right as he counted the forces assembling against him. Not all were tall or powerful looking, but there were many times more of them than there were of his angels.

Finally, he took a step back, and his followers did the same.

"This is not over," he said.

Vast wings beat the air as the angels flew off into the night.

* * *

"Next time you rescue me, please bring someone with wings," Damon said as they walked along the road back towards Durham, the sky starting to grow light ahead of them. They had left behind most of the demons, Damon giving them orders to watch the mages' base and trail Oldfield if she left. But Eldervain had insisted on leading them home, saying that he knew the best way for them to go.

"As you command, oh Master." The demon bobbed his head in a motion that managed to be both sincere and mocking. "But is it truly wings you want, or might you prefer a tank?"

"Why a tank?" Damon asked.

"Because we are about to get caught up in a battle."

As Eldervain spoke, gunfire erupted from the hillside ahead of them. There was a roar of artillery and a screech-ing sound, then a series of explosions shattered the countryside to their right.

"What the hell?" Ines flung herself at Damon, knocking him to the ground and landing on top of him. Shrapnel hissed past, and dirt pattered down around them.

"An ambush," Eldervain explained as he hit the ground, his face only inches from hers, the slumped skin unsettling even in the pre-dawn gloom. "The Scots have tracked a convoy carrying the royalist commander, and now—"

There was a roar as armored vehicles rushed along the road next to which they were lying. Bullets rattled off armor plates. An explosion tore up the road between the two leading vehicles, tossing both onto their sides. Others screeched to a halt, guns blazing through their windows.

"You did this on purpose, didn't you?" Damon snarled.

"Where better to recharge your powers, Young Master?" Eldervain said, his eyes sparkling at the pain and fear all around them. "Or would you prefer that your girlfriend cut her own flesh again?"

Ines's arm, freshly bandaged with a sleeve of Damon's shirt, throbbed with pain. She didn't want to go through that again, but this seemed far worse.

"I'm going to bloody kill you," Damon said. "As soon as we get out of here."

Rolling out from under Ines, he drew his watch and started muttering incantations.

"Wait," she said. An idea was unfolding in her mind. "Eldervain might be mad, but so is this. With so many other threats, can we afford to let humans keep tearing each other apart?"

"Can we stop them?" Damon asked doubtfully.

"Perhaps." Ines looked at the shattered convoy and the twenty or thirty soldiers taking shelter around it. "How many people can you freeze time for?"

* * *

"All right, you've got my attention." The Scottish general was a short man with a round face and an old-fashioned moustache. He faced Ines, Damon, and Eldervain from thirty feet away while his men kept their guns trained on the strange visitors.

It had taken over an hour to get him here. The whole while, Damon had kept time frozen around the English convoy. Even using all the pain of the men caught in the battle, all the fear of those caught in the ambush, and all the hate the demons had stirred for miles around, he was straining at his limits to keep the spell in place. Sweat streamed from his brow, and his body shook as he knelt at the edge of the spell.

In front of him, the thirty men of the convoy were frozen in time. They were still caught in the early moments of the battle, guns raised, eyes wide, looking around as they tried to find their enemies. The Scottish soldiers looked at them, and at Damon, with incredulity that bordered on fear—a little more fuel to keep the spell going. Their guns were raised, and if this went wrong, then there wasn't enough power left to stop them firing.

Ines really hoped that this didn't go wrong.

"My name is Ines Salgado," she began. "Are you General McCluskey?"

"Aye, that I am," the general said. "So we both know what I'm doing here. But what's your business, young lady?

I dinnae think you're old enough to be commanding soldiers."

"Looks old enough to command me," a soldier said, to sniggers from the others nearby.

Ines blushed then cringed, suddenly remembering stories of the terrible things soldiers sometimes did to women in times of war.

"I'm warning you, Captain Alexander, I've a daughter that age," McCluskey said. "I dinnae take kindly to such talk about a wee lass."

"Sorry, sir," the soldier said, hanging his head.

"Not to me, you idiot. To her."

"Sorry, ma'am," the soldier said, looking at Ines.

Bewildered, she just nodded.

"Back to business," General McCluskey said. "Who are you, Ines Salgado? What do you represent?"

"I'm a leader, like you," she said, trying to sound as if she believed it. "You've seen the strange things happening in the world. You have to know that this war has come from more than ordinary politics."

"Aye, that I do," McCluskey said, looking at Eldervain.

"The people I lead are trying to fix what's broken," Ines said. "To end this strangeness. To protect human beings from the creatures that have been doing so much harm."

"Do you not think soldiers can do that, young lady?" McCluskey said.

"Of course not," Eldervain rasped, waving his long arms. "We are the hosts of Hell and Heaven, beings beyond your darkest nightmares and brightest dreams. We have powers beyond your imagining. We are not—"

His words were cut short by a gunshot. The demon toppled to the ground, green blood spurting from his ruined knee.

McCluskey slid his pistol back into its holster.

Amazement crossed Ines's face. She hadn't thought that could happen. Judging by the looks on the faces of the soldiers, they were equally shocked, though more amused than she was.

She couldn't let surprise throw her now.

"You've fought them," she said.

McCluskey bobbed his head from side to side. "Not often, and not well, but aye, we have."

"Then you've seen the harm they can do," she said.

"Aye." For a moment, he turned a look of hatred upon the demon.

"You can see that I have access to powers you don't. I also have a plan to end all of this chaos. But while you keep fighting, it's hard for me to carry out that plan. My people are constantly at risk of getting caught up in the war.

"That's why I'm here now. Field Marshal Brancepeth-Holmes is caught within my colleague's magic. In a minute, we're going to release him. If you're willing to negotiate a truce, then we'll release him into your custody. You'll have the advantage in negotiations, as long as you stop fighting them and instead help us out.

"Alternatively, when he releases that spell, my colleague can turn it on you instead. You'll be frozen, and we'll hand you over to the English royalists in return for their support.

"So which will it be?"

McCluskey looked from her to the English commander frozen in time behind a tank. Then he turned his gaze upon Damon, sweating and straining to keep the spell in place.

"I'm not sure that laddie can keep this up much longer," the general said. "Never mind turn it on me and mine."

Ines swallowed. This was the moment she had most feared—the Scot seeing through her bluff. Should she give up and hope for the best? It was a terrible chance to take.

Someone had to take a chance.

"Are you willing to take that risk?" she asked, looking McCluskey in the eye. "Given what you stand to gain?"

"I suppose not." He smiled and stepped forward, hand extended. "All right, Ines Salgado, you have a deal."

One by one, Damon released the English soldiers from the spell, letting the Scots take them into custody. Last was the field marshal, a towering man with a grey beard and fury in his eyes.

As the two commanders sat on the hood of an armored car, talking truce under her watchful eye, Ines couldn't help but stare at McCluskey.

He had crippled a demon. Even now, as an English medic reluctantly helped him to splint his leg, Eldervain was moaning about the experience. If McCluskey could do that, then was Ines's ability to hurt demons and angels so very special?

Was she really as unique as Shaw thought?

CHAPTER 19
At Last

Every time Ines thought that her life could not get more surreal, something happened to prove her wrong. It was usually just a moment, an image that slapped her in the brain and reminded her that this was not what normal life looked like.

This morning, it was the sight of Damon, her best friend from school and sort-of-maybe-boyfriend, huddled in conversation with half a dozen assorted demons in front of a tank.

"This is mental," Captain Alexander said. Six foot two, broad shouldered, square jawed and blond haired, he looked as different from General McCluskey as any soldier could while wearing the same uniform. But he was the man McCluskey had left in charge of helping Ines with this operation as the general and most of his troops led the captive English away.

"You get used to it," Ines said, trying to sound more confident and in command than she felt.

Alexander let out a long breath.

"Not sure I ever will," he said. "More credit to you."

Damon walked over.

"A lot of the mages are out of the pub," he said. "The imps think they went on some sort of supply run. No one saw Oldfield leave, so we'll have to face her, but other than that, this seems like the perfect time to strike."

To Ines, Oldfield's presence just made it more perfect. Her desire to confront the minister was almost as great as the longing to rescue her mother.

"Are you sure you won't stay behind?" Damon pointed at her injured arm. Thanks to the soldiers, it was now stitched up and properly bandaged, but ordinary painkillers could only do so much to manage the effect of the wound.

"I'll be fine," she said, this time more confident. "Let's do this."

Rumiel was waiting for them behind the brow of the hill. As a tank rumbled up the road and began rolling down towards the pub, the angel took Ines and Damon beneath his arms and swept them up into the air.

From up above, Ines watched soldiers, demons, and mages closing in from every direction. Bullets and magic flew. There were bangs as explosives hit doors, and an almighty crashing as the tank smashed a hole in the front wall.

"Now!" she shouted.

Rumiel swept down towards the roof of the pub. A bolt of black energy shot from Damon's hands, and the tiles below them aged and crumbled before their eyes. The remains disintegrated as Rumiel slammed into them, and the three friends landed in a cloud of dust in a top-floor hallway.

The hall was lined with doors, each with a number on it—bedrooms for paying guests.

A door swung open, and a blast of magic shot out. Ines flung herself forward, winced as her arm hit the ground, rolled beneath the magic, and sprang up just in front of a mage, knocking him out cold with a single punch.

"Glorious work, Ines Salgado!" Rumiel laughed excitedly and swept her off her feet, drawing her close.

"Hey!" Damon snapped. "Get off of her!"

"What ails you?" Rumiel asked, still grinning as he turned to Damon. His arm lay around Ines's shoulder.

"What ails me is that we... That Ines and I..." Damon pressed his hand against his brow. "I can't believe I'm saying this now, but I've had enough. Ines and I, in Manchester, we... Stuff happened, all right?"

"What is he talking about?" Rumiel looked at her.

"Not now," Ines hissed desperately.

"When we kissed on the train," Rumiel said, "was that not—"

"You kissed on the train?" Damon looked at her in hurt and confusion. "What the hell?"

"Enough!" Ines said. "Yes, I've done things I shouldn't, but we're in the middle of a rescue, so can we please save this for—"

More blasts of crude magic hurtled towards them from the end of the corridor. Damon held up his hand, catching one of the blasts in a bowl of blackness, then flung it back where it had come from.

"This isn't over," he said, glaring angrily at Ines. Then he strode off towards the enemy, watch held out in front of him, chanting furiously.

Rumiel didn't even speak. He just drew his sword and charged.

"Boys," Ines spat, angry and frustrated. "It's always about them."

A tugging at her hoodie made her look down. She had expected to see someone there, but instead, the cloth seemed to be moving of its own accord.

Feeling in her pocket, she found the ward that her father had made. It was pressing against the other material, lifting up like a piece of metal drawn towards a magnet.

"Are you leading me somewhere?" Ines asked.

She pulled the ward out of her pocket and let it go. The scrap of cloth hung in the air for a moment then shot across the corridor and slammed into a door.

"Is Mum here?" Ines asked excitedly. "Is that what you're trying to say?"

The cloth did not respond.

The door was locked, the handle completely unmoving. Putting all her strength into it, Ines flung herself against the door, but it wouldn't give, and her bruised flesh hurt too much to try again. Looking around for anything that might help, she spotted a fire extinguisher hanging on the wall. With this improvised battering ram, she smashed at the wood around the door handle until it splintered and then, with a drawn-out crack, flew open.

Beyond was a small room. There was a bed to one side, a narrow wardrobe, and a sink in the corner. In the room's only chair, her arms and legs bound with both duct tape and shimmering magic, sat Ines's mother.

"Mum!" Ines wrapped her arms around her mother, tears running down her cheeks. "I'm so glad to see you."

Carefully, she pulled the duct tape away from her mum's mouth.

"Ines, sweetheart," Julie Salgado said, eyes wide. "What are you doing here?"

"Rescuing you."

Ines didn't know much about magical bonds, but she knew that she had one tool for countering magic, especially magic that threatened her and her family. Picking up the ward, she pressed it against the magic tying her mother in place. Each bond in turn dissolved at the ward's touch. But as it did so, the magic burned the ward, so that by the end, Ines was holding little more than a square of charred cloth.

With her knife, she made easy work of the duct tape. Soon, her mum was free.

They stepped out into the corridor, Ines's mum leaning on her for support. She seemed weak and disoriented.

"Rumiel!" Ines shouted.

The angel appeared at the end of the corridor, sword in hand.

"Quick," Ines said. "She needs help. Fly her out of here."

Rumiel didn't say anything. He didn't even look Ines in the eye. But he walked over, lifted her mother in his arms, and flew out through the hole in the ceiling.

So that was how it was going to be. If Ines was going to suffer the fallout from today, then she was at least going to get the most out of it.

She was going after Oldfield.

The mage she had knocked out still lay on the floor of one of the bedrooms. Ines hauled him to his feet, planted him in a chair, and slapped him across the face.

With a groan, he opened his eyes and looked up at her. One of his hands moved as if to cast a spell, but Ines grabbed it and pinned it in place against the wall, her strength and her fury greater than his.

"Where's Oldfield?" she growled, letting her voice go low, the anger oozing out of her.

"Don't know," the mage said. His eyes flicked nervously back and forth as he licked at the blood slowly dribbling from his lip.

"You're lying," Ines said. She slapped him again. "Where is she?"

"Still don't know," the mage replied. "Wouldn't tell you if I did."

"Tell me." Ines punched him in the gut.

The mage laughed.

"Screw you," he groaned.

"Tell me!"

Ines yanked him out of the seat and slammed him against the wall. There was a crack as his head hit, and he went cross-eyed.

Downstairs, the sounds of fighting grew louder. More gunshots, more blows and shouts, more hissing and crackling of magic.

"Tell me!" Ines flung the man to the floor and crouched over him, pinning him there as she slapped his head back and forth.

"Tell me!" she yelled as he groaned and his eyes rolled back in his head.

Footsteps came running up the stairs.

"Ines, we have to get going." Hema appeared in the doorway.

Her look of shock brought Ines back to her senses. She saw the man lying unconscious and battered in front of her, his blood smearing her knuckles. She realised how crazed she must look.

"I..." She didn't know what to say.

"Come on," Hema said, helping her to her feet. "Someone's waiting for you."

* * *

In the back of an armored car, bumping along the shell-shattered road to Durham, Ines laid her head against her mother's shoulder. Short dark hair tickled her cheek. The space smelled of sweat, gunfire, and old boots. Every turn the vehicle took sent them jolting back and forth in their seat. But she didn't care. She had her mum at last.

Julie Salgado wrapped her daughter's hand in her own.

"I'm so proud of you, Ines," she said. "You've been doing great things."

"You don't understand," Ines said. "I've ruined so much. Damon and Rumiel and... and... And I nearly beat a man to death just now."

"Hush." Mum stroked her cheek, just as she had when Ines was little. "Nobody is perfect. Nobody gets everything right.

But I'm here for you now. Whatever's gone wrong, we can get through it together."

Ines clung to her mother.

"I love you, Mum," she said.

"I love you too, Ines."

CHAPTER 20
No Barriers to Mercy

The notes and diagrams were incom-prehensible to Ines. Her mum, Marklew, and the mages working with them were using some notation she didn't under-stand, strings of symbols representing magical concepts, strung together like lines of esoteric algebra. Even the bits written in English didn't mean much to her, with their talk of ley lines, morphic resonances, and teleological constants. Every wall of the room was covered in the stuff, sheets of paper plastered over each other as they ran out of space. The meeting table was littered with notepaper, old books, laptops, and empty coffee cups. The conversation was lively, the mages deeply engaged in the work of planning a new Barrier of Mercy, but she wasn't part of it.

Loath as she was to be away from her mum, Ines knew that she didn't belong here. The mages were slipping into familiar ways of working that she wasn't part of.

Unnoticed, she slipped out of the room.

Walking down the corridor, she passed a group of demons conspiring in a corner. Seeing a human approach, they cackled and rubbed their hands together. She just walked on past.

At the end of the corridor, the windows of a stairwell looked out of the student accommodation block onto a car park. The strangeness of seeing angels hanging around in mundane places had finally passed, but still, she was struck by what she saw out there. Half a dozen angels knelt before Rumiel, undertaking a ritual of commitment to him as head of their host.

Everyone was falling into familiar patterns.

Slow footsteps approached up the stairwell. To Ines's delight, Tamsin Shaw rounded the corner, supported by a walking stick on one side and Hema on the other.

"Shaw!" Ines rushed down the steps and hugged her friend. Shaw wobbled under the impact but stayed upright.

"Ines." Shaw hugged her back with her free arm. "Please, call me Tamsin."

"Okay." Ines smiled. Leading the Earthly Host had made her feel grown up, but it was moments like this that made her feel like an equal with the adults in her life.

"Could you help me up to the meeting room?" Shaw asked.

Together, the three of them headed up the stairs and along the corridor. It was slow going. Shaw was still weak, and her movements were hesitant. The paleness of her skin almost made the scars on her cheek vanish.

Despite the pain, her voice and spirit were as strong as ever. She listened attentively as Ines told her about events while she had been in the hospital.

"I have news as well," Shaw said.

As they entered the meeting room, the mages looked up from their work for the first time all day. Applause filled the room. As it died down, Shaw nodded her head towards Ines's mum.

"Dr. Salgado," Shaw said stiffly. "Good to have you with us."

"Good to be here, Miss Shaw," Ines's mum replied. "And to see you so well."

"Thank you." Shaw eased herself into a seat. "I have exciting news. We've done a head count, and the majority of mages from the Ministry are now in our group. I've reached out to the Scots and the royalists, and we have permission from both those governments to appoint a new minister." She looked at Mum. "Obviously, we'll need to talk about who it's going to be."

"I don't think so." Julie Salgado held out her hand. "Congratulations, Minister Shaw. I hear that the appointment is well earned."

Tension Ines had barely noticed eased out of Shaw, and the new minister smiled as she shook Mum's hand.

* * *

"I need three people to go gather some information," Ines said, looking around at the mages in the common room.

They looked at each other, then one raised a hand.

"We should check with Minister Shaw," he said. "Before we do anything."

"Yesterday, you'd do what I asked," Ines said.

"Yesterday, we didn't have a minister."

"Fine," Ines snapped. "Check quickly, then come find me."

She stamped her way out of the building. This was stupid. Things were going well—why did she feel as though they were falling apart?

Around the back of their base was a small garden—an un-mowed lawn, a couple of trees, and a wooden bench. She flung herself down on the bench and sat glaring at the greenery, fingers drumming against the seat.

There were things they needed to do. Ways of fighting the supernatural forces overrunning their world. She had plans for that, and now people weren't listening. Did they want to be put in danger?

People could be so stupid.

"Ines?" It was her mother's voice, calling from around the corner.

"I'm here, Mum," she shouted back.

Julie Salgado appeared at the side of the garden. She had abandoned the tatty Ministry suit in which Ines had found her, switching to black trousers and blouse. Her short hair hung neatly to either side of her face.

"How are you doing, sweetheart?" Mum said as she sat down beside Ines.

"Frustrated," Ines replied. "There's so much awfulness out there. People like Oldfield who hurt you and Dad and Toby. Angels like Michael, killing people because he doesn't agree with them. Demons feeding off hate and pain and fear. It makes me so mad. I want to punch them all in the face, to kick them while they're down, to show them why they shouldn't mess with me and the people I love."

A little brown bird landed in the overgrown grass. Its head bobbed up and down as it pecked at the ground, eventually pulling up a long worm. Then, with a flutter of wings, it flew away.

"Has anyone told you what happened to Sarah Oldfield, Elizabeth's daughter?" Mum asked.

"No." Ines shook her head. "Why?"

"This was when you were younger," Mum said. "Too young to hear about such horrible things. But it was what motivated your father and I to make sure you knew how to protect yourself.

"Elizabeth had Sarah when she was young. She loved her dearly, but she struggled with being a mother, and I think that made her feel a little guilty already, as if what she was doing wasn't good enough.

"Then there was an incident at an underground station. Elizabeth was taking Sarah home from a trip to the zoo when demons attacked. I don't know what they had been sent to do, but they sensed Elizabeth's power, and they latched onto something in her. She had to fight them off. One of them hurt Sarah. Hurt her badly. She's been on life support in hospital ever since.

"For a long time, Elizabeth was bitter about the way supernatural forces had hurt her family. It's what made her so ambitious, and so determined to grasp more power. I thought that she had moved past it, until all of this happened.

"Don't let anger and bitterness become the things that drive you, Ines. Nothing good lies down that path."

Ines wiped the tears running down her cheeks. She wrapped her arms around her mother.

"I won't," she said with a sniff. "I'm sorry."

"You have nothing to be sorry about." Mum hugged her back. "Nothing that's happened is your fault. It's what you choose to do about it that matters."

Ines disentangled herself and rubbed her sleeve across her face, wiping away the tears.

"I want to find a better way to be," she said. "But it's hard."

"I know, honey."

"Ines, come quick!" someone yelled in the distance. "You need to hear this!"

* * *

The cell had once been a storage basement. The only decoration on the walls was that required for the spells cast here—symbols carved into the concrete, glowing with magical power, turning mere physical barriers into a magical restraint strong enough to hold an angel. Most of the light came not from those symbols but from the prisoner himself, his body glowing with the mystical energy of heaven.

"There has been a massacre," Ines said. "Did you know that?"

She stood in front of Sanctus, arms folded across her body. She was trying to hold herself steady, to sound calm and commanding. But being alone in the cell with this creature, facing him up close, brought back memories of their previous encounters. Looking up at his square face and muscled body, she couldn't help but shake with fear.

"This is what humans do to each other," Sanctus said with a shrug. "What you do in war."

"It was not humans who committed the massacre," Ines said. "It was your kind. Your master. Michael and the angels of the Blazing Host."

"It is our place to bring judgement," Sanctus said. "Your place to accept it."

"The people they massacred were soldiers," Ines said. "Scottish soldiers. People fighting for their country, for what they thought was right. I'd met some of them. They had families and friends back home. They were trying to do right by them. They were good people."

"Good people do not face the wrath of Heaven," Sanctus said. "As you will when I am free."

Ines unfolded her arms, sliding a knife from her sleeve.

"I hear that you can't use your powers in here," she said. "That you can't summon a weapon."

It was the first time she had ever seen him show fear. Never mind that he was twice as large as her. For the first time, Sanctus was feeling vulnerable, and his face showed it.

"You just can't stop yourselves, can you?" Ines said, tapping the flat of the blade against her hand. All the hate and pain she felt flowed out through her voice. "You kill and you destroy because that's all you've ever known. All you can think to do. The most powerful beings in the world, turning their strength upon those weaker than them. You claim to be the forces of good, but all you bring is evil."

Sanctus's eyes never moved off the knife blade.

"Do it," he whispered. "You have judged me, though you have not the right. I will never waver in my faith. I will never bow to your commands. So end this, as you clearly intend."

"That is why I came here," Ines said.

Reaching out with the knife, she ran its tip down one of the symbols on the wall. Steel scraped against concrete, and as the symbol was broken, the light of its magic died.

Around the room, other symbols dimmed.

Turning her back on Sanctus, desperately hoping that his surprise would give her the time she needed, Ines opened the door.

"Come with me," she said.

All the way up the stairs, she was terribly aware of the angel behind her—the thud of his footsteps, the light shining from a body far stronger than her own. All he had to do was grab her by the throat, and this would be over.

They emerged from another doorway at the top of the steps. In front of them, the car park in front of the Earthly Host's headquarters was full of people. Mages, angels, demons, Scottish soldiers, even a representative of the English royalists, looking uncomfortable standing beside his opponents despite their truce.

As Sanctus emerged, confusion still across his face, Ines clambered up onto the roof of a car, where everyone could see her.

"If I had followed my instincts, Sanctus would be dead," she declared loudly, letting her voice carry across the car park. "But I didn't. Because I don't have to be a slave to those instincts. None of us do.

"If you had followed the rules that bound you before, then many of you would not be here. You would still be following masters who order massacres or choose war over words, who believe that the way you come into this world should determine your place in it. But none of us have to follow those rules or those masters.

"We have choices now, choices that will shape each of us and the world we live in.

Being an angel does not mean that you have to pass terrible judgement. Being a demon does not mean that you have to choose cruelty and snivelling obedience to your lords. Being human does not mean blindly following generals, ministers, and those who think themselves better than us.

"We are free. Each act we take defines us as well as our world."

She held her knife in the air then slid it back into its place up her sleeve. Turning to face Sanctus, she spoke again.

"I choose not to be someone who kills a prisoner at my mercy. Instead, I am freeing you to make your own choice. Whether you side with us or with Michael, it will not happen because it was in your nature. It will be up to you."

She turned to face the crowd again.

"We chose to make a better world. Let's not lose our better selves along the way."

The crowd cheered as she leapt down from the car. Beside her, Sanctus stood uncertain, his wings half-unfurled.

Mum walked up to her.

"That was beautiful, sweetheart," she said, placing her hands on Ines's shoulders. "Oh my, you're shaking like a leaf!"

Ines shrugged.

"I chose to do that," she said. "But I couldn't choose to make it easy."

CHAPTER 21
When Angels Fall

Ines took a final drink from her bottle of water and then set it down in the doorway of a shop. She felt guilty about the litter then felt absurd for worrying about that when she was about to go to war. Despite the water, her mouth still felt dry.

The air crackled, and Hema appeared in the doorway.

"It worked," she said quietly.

"Then it's time." Ines raised her hand. Up and down the street, mages, demons, and even a couple of angels emerged from doorways or descended from rooftops. She lowered her hand, and as she began running up the street towards Palace Green, her strange army followed her.

She was a general now.

Late-afternoon shadows stretched across Palace Green, a dark congregation of flat shapes gathered before the great cathedral. The building's towers glowed with the last light of the day, becoming all the brighter against a sky of deep, glorious blue.

Nobody spoke as they raced across the green. The only sound accompanying their footsteps was that of fighting half a mile away—screams, shouts, and the occasional boom of Eldervain's hellish pistols. He and the imps had done their work. The angels had been drawn away from the cathedral.

Rumiel was fast in the air, but no one in their group was faster at a run than Ines. She was the first one to reach the open doors of the cathedral. Cold air soothed her sweaty skin as she stepped inside. Not a soul moved in the vast, echoing chamber of the house of worship.

"This way." She led them up the nave, around the choir seats, pulpit, and screen, to the entrance to the shrine of St. Cuthbert. There she stopped, caught by the memory of her last experience, muscles stiffening as she thought about heading up those steps.

"Don't worry, sweetheart." Mum hurried up to her. "We have this."

Julie Salgado headed fearlessly up those steps. Rumiel and Damon were behind her, each giving Ines a reassuring smile. Then followed the other demons, angels, and mages who would take part in the ritual to rebuild the Barrier of Mercy.

Chanting began. Ines stepped back, turning to face the others who were with her.

"Michael can't miss this," she said. "Get ready to buy the ritualists time."

A boom filled the cathedral. Dashing back towards the entrance, Ines saw melted glass and burning wood scattered across the floor, all that remained of the great doors and the tourist entrance area behind them. The archangel Michael stood amid the ruins, plate armor gleaming as if in full sunlight, angels pouring in behind him.

"Heretics!" he bellowed. "Heathens! Blasphemers! Prepare to face the wrath of His judgement!"

There was no time to think and only a moment to give commands. It was as they had expected. It was what Ines had prepared for.

"Team one, shield us!" she shouted. "Team two, open fire!"

As the angels rushed towards them, mages and demons began chanting together. Strands of dark and grey magic wove together, forming a barrier in front of them. Angelic arrows and spears hit this shield and exploded in showers of light.

To the right, more mages and demons raised their hands and began to chant. Instead of building a shield, they launched an attack. Bursts of light, balls of flame, and bolts of pure crackling magic hit the angels on that side. Some fell, while others charged forward with fresh resolve.

At the back of the angelic host stood Michael, bellowing orders at his followers. Sanctus stood at his right hand, watching warily, hands balled into fists at his sides.

That answered the question she had been fretting over since his release. Sanctus had chosen his path.

Powerful as the assembled magic casters were, the angels were powerful too. They slammed into the defensive barrier, some bouncing off it, others slicing through with blazing weapons.

"Team three, now!" Ines yelled.

From the left came three bright-white figures, angels of the Earthly Host. At their head was Helda, battle-axe raised above her head, blond hair flowing behind her, face a vision of fury. She screamed something in an ancient, guttural language that Ines couldn't understand then plowed her axe through the shoulder of one of the enemy.

Behind their angels came the rest of the mages and demons, those not suited to defense or to fighting at range. Creatures of spikes and claws. Imps whose heads were nothing but row upon row of teeth. Mages who could turn their fists to stone or leap and lunge as though they were made from the wind.

As the battle turned into a wild melee, Ines longed to join it. Not out of bloodlust, but out of the desperate need to be useful, an instinct that made her twitch to the core of her body.

But somebody needed to lead. Somebody needed to watch for what went wrong and step in to fix the problems. Somebody had to give orders.

"Simms, the flank," she shouted, sending mages to stop the angels surrounding them. "Githtor, pull back to the seats."

She had to shout so loudly over the battle noises that her throat felt as if it were being sandpapered. This, apparently, was the price of command.

A touch on her shoulder made her jump. A worried-looking mage stared at her.

"You need to see this," he said.

Reluctantly, Ines stepped away from the battlefield and followed the young mage—he couldn't have been more than five years older than her—around to Cuthbert's shrine. Gritting her teeth, she forced herself to follow him up the steps.

Her mother, Rumiel, Damon, and the rest stood in a circle around the shrine. The energy she had cast herself into before flowed around and through them, its path twisting with the magic emanating from their hands. It seemed to flow into channels then break free, rushing out and away. Their faces were strained, only Rumiel not drenched with sweat.

"It's not working," the young mage whispered. "The barrier is fighting back somehow. It refuses to be fixed."

One of the mages grunted and slumped to the ground. A blast of power shot out past him, exploding off the wall and knocking over two of the demons. Tattered strands of magic flailed like tentacles around the room.

For a moment, Ines froze, trapped between stubborn fixation on what she wanted and a terrible, realistic grasp on what was happening.

"Stop," she said reluctantly. "It's not working, and the angels are closing in. We have to retreat."

"We can make it work," Mum called out.

"Indeed, we can," Rumiel said, even as he sank to one knee.

"No, you can't," Ines said. "We have to go. Now."

She grabbed the nearest of them, a tall, willowy demon in a black dress, and pulled her out of the circle. As their magic collapsed, the others stepped back.

There was no time to worry about the lost opportunity. The sounds of fighting outside the shrine were growing more intense.

"Damon, Mum, make sure the rest of your team get out safely," Ines said. "Rumiel, you're with me."

"What mission would you have me undertake?" he asked, his flaming sword appearing in his hand.

"We're going to stop your old boss," Ines replied. In her head, there was more to that sentence. They would stop Michael, or they would die trying.

As they emerged from the shrine and back into the battle, she saw Michael entering the melee. He swung to the left and right with his sword, cutting down demons and mages alike. His wings beat powerfully behind him, knocking others aside.

Inspired by his presence, the Blazing Host pressed forward with strength and confidence. Some had taken to the air, stopping any demons who tried to fly past. The rest fought on the ground, forming a nearly impenetrable mass of holy blades and glowing shields. They were pressing the Earthly Host back. There was no way to the exit.

"Fly us in," Ines said.

Rumiel wrapped a strong arm around her, his warm body pressing against hers. With a single movement of his wings, he lifted them both into the air. They glided above the heads of the fighters, landing in the bloodstained space in front of Michael.

"The traitor and his pet," Michael sneered. His eyes, normally as cold and deadly as sharpened steel, were wild with rage. "I will take great pleasure in gutting you both at last." He raised a hand and beckoned to someone behind him. "Sanctus, your assistance."

Behind Michael, Sanctus stood unmoving, fists clenched at his sides.

"Sanctus?" Michael turned to his lieutenant with a snarl. Other angels around Sanctus watched them in confusion.

Sanctus looked from Michael to Ines and then back again.

"No," he said.

"Will you too defy the will of Heaven?" Michael said. "We are the strong. We are the righteous."

"That is what Lucifer thought," Sanctus said, his face contorted with something close to grief. "How much better the world in which the strong and the righteous also allowed themselves doubt."

"Then I will deal with you later," Michael snapped. He turned back to face Ines and Rumiel. "Let me first cut away the cancer before it spreads further."

Many of the angels, seeing the confrontation at their core, had backed away from the fight. Given their moment, Helda and her comrades cut a way through along one side, letting Damon and Mum lead the barrier team to safety. But in the center of the cathedral, two armies still stood facing each other, waiting to see how their leaders would fare.

Rumiel was the first to attack. Sword raised, he dived at his former commander, wings driving him forwards in a powerful lunge. Michael twisted his blade and flicked Rumiel's aside with casual ease then slammed into Rumiel with his shoulder, knocking him to the ground. Both angels flapped their wings, Rumiel rising and Michael descending upon him.

Their movements became a blur of blades and feathers. Rumiel fought his way to his feet and for a moment seemed to gain the advantage, only for Michael to slam him back against one of the cathedral's great pillars. There was a sound of scraping stone, and dust tumbled from above.

Rumiel ducked a strike that took a wedge out of the stone. His counterattack sent Michael flying back, crashing through two demons and slamming an angel against the wall. The combatants' blades clashed and twirled, the two of them launching frenzied assaults that filled the whole building with the sound of steel upon steel. A wild blow caught a mage who stood too close, severing his hand in a spray of blood.

Fascination turned to fear. The onlookers went from backing off to rushing out of the building, trying to get away from combatants fixated only on themselves.

Ines and Sanctus remained to watch, he with an expression of dead-eyed indifference, she with her guts knotted in tension. She wanted to help Rumiel, but they were moving too fast. Any time she saw a way in, it vanished before she could act. Her hand tightened around the handle of her knife, but once again, she found herself frustratingly excluded from the action.

It could not last forever. Rumiel was strong, but Michael was stronger. The junior angel began to tire, his attacks becoming slower and less certain. Michael drove him back until he was pressed against the wall and struggling to defend himself.

It was now or never. Her heart pounding, Ines ran and leapt, landing on Michael's back. She wrapped her arm around his throat and her legs around his waist, clinging desperately as he tried to shake her off. Raising the knife, she plunged it into the one part of his body not protected by armor—the side of his face.

Michael's scream was terrible to hear, a sound so piercing it made Ines's ears hurt and her body shake with grief. The blade protruding from his face, Michael dropped his sword and reached back, grasping her with both hands. He wrenched her off of him and held her above his head, ready to smash her against the ground.

Then he screamed again. Looking down, she saw Rumiel gripping his sword with both hands. The blade was thrust almost the whole way through Michael's chest.

It was a blow that would have killed any mortal creature. Even Michael, archangel of the Blazing Host, staggered back from it, dropping Ines. A scraping sound echoed around them as the sword slid out of his armor. Light poured like blood from the wound.

Flapping his wings weakly, Michael rose, wobbling, into the air. Gathering speed, he crashed through a stained-glass window and disappeared into the dusk sky.

"You are my absolute hero," Ines said, grinning up at Rumiel.

"And you mine," he said, offering a hand to help her up. He frowned. "We failed. The Barrier has not been restored."

Frustration rose inside Ines at the reminder. Then she looked at the shattered stained glass lying beneath the broken window, and she smiled grimly.

"Not yet," she said.

CHAPTER 22
Mortals

As she emerged from the cathedral, Ines found a vast crowd watching her. Angels, demons, mages—all waiting to hear what had happened. The remnants of the Blazing Host stood off to one side, Sanctus and others standing uncertain now that their leader was gone. To her right, a group of soldiers were coming into Palace Green, allies arriving to see if she had succeeded and if she needed help.

Standing on the low wall at the edge of the cathedral grounds would still leave her shorter than half the beings there. Making the most of her agility and sense of balance, she leapt onto the top of a gravestone and stood, looking around at them all.

"We defeated Michael!" she shouted.

Cheers and applause washed over her in a great wave. Someone started chanting her name, and soon, the whole crowd was joining in.

"Ines! Ines! Ines!" they cried out.

She smiled. This part of leadership felt good.

Then she looked across that sea of faces again, and her heart sank. The mages looked pale and drawn, many of them bruised and bandaged. The soldiers were stiff with tension, their clothes stained with blood and mud, their uniforms decorated with bandages and tears. The angels and demons too were injured, their bodies sagging with their spirits.

Her people were on their last legs. They had fought and bled, given their all to see the barrier restored, and still, they had failed. How could she ask more of them?

As she mustered her thoughts, she looked beyond them, at the surrounding buildings. A medieval alms house that had once housed a cafe was now a burnt-out shell. Buildings at the end of the green had shattered windows and graffiti-stained walls. The pavement in front of the burnt-out building was a string of craters.

This beautiful historical place had been reduced to ruin. She didn't dare to imagine how much worse the world beyond was, torn as it was by wars, rioting, and all manner of destruction.

Her spirits heavy over what she had to say, she raised her hands. Slowly, the crowd fell silent.

"The ritual failed," Ines said, her voice cracking from the pain in her throat and in her heart. "The Barrier of Mercy is still down."

There were disappointed murmurs.

"I know that you're tired," she continued. "Many of you are injured, some badly. And that's why I'm going to ask even more of you now.

"The longer we wait to restore the Barrier, the worse things will become. The more of us will be injured or killed. The more of the world around us will be ruined. If we carry on like this, then soon, there will be no world left to save, and no one to save it.

"You want to rest. I understand that. I do too. But please, stay with me here now. We'll find another way to do this. We'll make it right."

This time, there was no loud cheering, just uncertain clapping. That would have to do.

Jumping down from her perch, Ines looked around for her experts on the Barrier.

They were waiting for her by the entrance to the cathedral. Mostly mages, with her mother at the center of their discussions. Shaw was among them, looking pale and strained, Hema hovering by her shoulder, watching her carefully and ready to catch her if she stumbled. Marklew was present too—he had insisted on witnessing the outcome of the ritual from the far side of the green, even if he had no magic to contribute. Alongside them were Damon and Eldervain, the sinister demon's trouser leg torn and stained from his injury against the Scots. Lastly, there was Rumiel, always Rumiel, standing tall and proud as a statue. He understood little of magical theory, but they needed an angel to agree to any scheme.

"We need a plan," Ines said. "Another way to try to fix the Barrier. And we need it now."

"It can't be done," one of the mages said. "It's in the nature of the magics. The demonic, angelic, and magely forces refuse to be bound together in any lasting way."

"Why not?" Ines asked.

As soon as the answers started, she regretted asking. The mages produced a stream of theory and jargon in which every other word was meaningless to her, every sentence indecipherable. Even Mum was spouting technical gibberish, reminding Ines of how much better Dad had always been at explaining things.

Bewildered and frustrated, she turned her gaze to Damon, who returned a calm, reassuring smile.

"Think of it as like oil and water," he said. "The parts are incompatible. You can mix them together, but as soon as you stop doing that, they'll come apart. We can't make a lasting barrier this way."

Even as he maintained his reassuring tone, his shoulders sagged. The others looked equally despondent.

"And here I thought myself among the experts," Eldervain said with a sneer. "The wise women and men who have kept us mere creatures in our place. Surely you have the answers the world needs?"

"I have an answer for you," a mage said, gathering magic in her fists. "And it's to send you back to Hell before your kind wreak any more havoc."

"Their kind?" Rumiel scowled. "You are the ones who tore open the Barrier. The world was safe and stable until—"

"Safe and stable?" the mage said. "Under your thumb, you mean."

"At least I was—"

"Enough!" Ines snapped. Shocked faces turned to look at her. She lowered her voice. "Everyone here is counting on you. If all you do is argue, then so will they, and that won't end well."

She looked at them each in turn—Damon, Rumiel, Mum, Shaw, Hema, and all the others brought together to fix the Barrier. Some she knew and loved, others she had barely met. But she saw the good in all of them, and how frustration was turning that to bitterness and rage.

"You can find a way to do this," she said. "I know you can. Not because of your magic, that strange strand of power in each of you. But because of who you are as people. The parts of you that are mortal, living things, and that represent the best of what we can be. Wise people. Strong people. People who just want to make the world a better place so that you can find your own happy spot within it."

Beside her, Shaw reached back a hand and caught hold of Hema's fingers.

"Oil and water couldn't be mixed until someone invented emulsions," Ines said, pulling out one of the few things she remembered from chemistry class. "Demon power, angel power, and mage power couldn't be combined before, but you can find a way. You can find it through that simple strand of mortal life that already binds you together. I believe in you."

Damon smiled and gave her a nod. She smiled back, her spirits lifting, as the mages turned to each other and started to talk.

"I'm sorry, sweetheart." Mum's voice cut across the conversations. "But that's just not the way this works."

Ines stared at her in surprise. "What do you mean?"

"I mean that you can't just wish this better," Mum said. "That's not the way magic works. Where things like this are concerned, you have to rely on the magic. Understand it. Use it. Bend it to your will, by all means. But, ultimately, follow its rules. No amount of pretty speeches and self-belief is going to change that."

Sadness and disappointment filled Ines. Not just to have her ideas fall apart, but to be criticized like this in front of everyone, by her mother, one of the people she trusted most in the world. The sadness in Mum's eyes didn't make it any less hurtful.

Ines felt anger as well. After all, she had fought mages, demons, and angels. She hadn't achieved that through magic. There was nothing special about her, and she knew it. She had achieved it all in the same way that she had brought this army together, this mingling of forces from every side. She had done it because she believed in herself and in the people around her. Because she had the willingness and the determination to fight. Because, at the end of the day, an ordinary mortal with an ordinary knife made from nothing more than the ordinary material of the world she lived in could take the head off a demon or rip open the guts of an angel.

She could do all that, and if she could, then so could others.

The mortal realm could master the magical, if they had the will to do it.

"You're wrong," she said. "We've all been wrong this whole time. We've made this about angels, demons, and mages. Doing that, we've ignored the people this affects the most. The people most deeply tied to the world this barrier will be built around. Ordinary, non-magical people."

Something flickered in Marklew's eyes, and he smiled.

"Yes," he said. "Keep going. I think you're on to something."

"The barrier is meant to protect the mortal world, so why shouldn't it be bound by it?" Ines waved her hands, the intensity of her feelings pouring out in a wave of enthusiasm. "Put an ordinary human in there too. Put me into the ritual. Use humanity to bind these magical powers in protecting the human world.

"In fact, don't just use me. Use all of us. Wise people like Marklew. Brave people like the soldiers here to protect us. This new barrier we're building is about defending humanity from the worst of what lies beyond. Let's use the best of humanity to do that."

"I really don't think—" Mum began.

"I do," Marklew said. "I've studied the theory, and I think this can work."

"I agree," Shaw said. "It's a good idea, and that shouldn't surprise any of us— Ines hasn't had a bad one yet."

"Let's do it," Hema said.

The others nodded their agreement.

"So now what, oh mighty leader?" Eldervain said with an exaggerated bow. "Will you lead your whole army into the cathedral?"

"No," Ines said. "You will—you, Sanctus, Shaw, and whoever's in charge of those soldiers."

"Such politics," Eldervain said. "Such an old head on a young body. You would have made a fine demon."

"Er, thanks," Ines said.

As the crowd started heading into the cathedral, Mum came to stand in front of Ines.

"I hope that you're right, sweetheart," she said, though her face showed how small her faith in the plan was. "For all our sakes."

"I'm not a little girl anymore, Mum," Ines said. "I've learned a lot in the past few months. And if this fails, then that's one more lesson to build on."

Her mother nodded and headed into the cathedral.

A hand squeezed Ines's shoulder. She turned to find Damon standing beside her.

"The best of humanity," he said, quoting back her own words. "You know that's who you are, right?"

"I'm not the best," she said. "I was just in the right place at the right time."

"And ridiculously humble too." Damon shook his head. "You'll always be the best to me."

He bent to kiss her on the cheek. On an impulse, she turned toward the kiss, so that their lips touched for one brief, electrifying moment.

"Let's go save the world," she whispered in his ear.

CHAPTER 23
Time to Choose

Marklew and Shaw stood in the doorway of the cathedral, directing people as they entered. Behind them, research mages were leafing through papers and frantically scribbling notes, gathering ingredients, and casting preparatory spells. The whole scale of the ritual felt far grander than what they had tried before.

"Through there," Marklew said, pointing her through a doorway at the near end of the cathedral. "You will be proceeding in at the start of the ritual. It represents—well, never mind what it represents. Shaw can lead the way."

Through the doorway, Ines found herself in a chapel cooler and quieter than the rest of the church. She passed what looked like a dining table made from a single slab of black stone. She brushed her fingers across the old, cold rock, realizing as she did so that it must be the tomb of someone important.

"His name was Bede." Rumiel stood in the center of the room, wings spread behind him, still looking as majestic as the day they had met. "A scholar who died centuries before you were born." He looked at the tomb and smiled. "He was a fine man. I liked the way he laughed."

Ines found her whole attention drawn to Rumiel. The chapel was beautiful and tranquil, but without other people to distract her, she found the angel drew all of her attention.

She remembered the moments of intimacy they had shared. Fond looks, held gazes, kisses as sudden and powerful as lightning from a clear sky. His words swirled through her mind. Kind things he had said, and cruel ones when he sided with Michael. Those last words about Bede, a reminder of how different their lives were in every way. He might look like a teenager, but he was older than this building. For the next year, Ines would still be a child in the eyes of the law, while he had lived since before that law was written.

Rumiel was beautiful, strong, and good. He had the face and the body of a model. He was so perfect that it felt unreal.

"There is something we must discuss," he said, stepping around the tomb to stand beside her.

"I suppose," she said, hoping that it was about the ritual. Important as her feelings for him were, she squirmed at the thought of talking about them.

"This business is nearing its end," Rumiel said. "As you so wisely said, if we do not succeed soon, then it will be too late. It is possible that neither of us will live to see another night."

Reluctantly, Ines nodded her agreement.

"Should we fall, then what I say now matters not," Rumiel continued. "It is but memory, more dust in a shattered world.

"But should we succeed, I need to choose a path. Without Michael, the Blazing Host are lost. I could lead them, return to our place in Heaven and continue God's great works, doing so more kindly than in the past. There is a place for me in reshaping the forces of Heaven, should I wish it.

"Or I could remain here, with you. Make a life in this world, as part of the new order that will rise from all we have been through. An order you will play some part in shaping, I am sure, Ines Salgado. But I would only choose this path to be with you. I can only choose it if you wish to be with me."

He took her hand in both of his.

"Which will it be?" he asked, staring deep into her eyes.

"I can't decide your future for you," she said, her whole body trembling.

"Then choose your own," he said. "You know the choice of which I speak. Which of us will it be?"

Ines's head was a whirl of conflicting desires, a spinning, tangled mass that blocked out all rational thought. Panic made her clench, tightening her grip on Rumiel's hand.

"I've never..." she began but couldn't complete the sentence. "I don't know how to..."

Footsteps made her turn. Shaw walked into the chapel, supported by Damon.

"We're joining you for this procession," Damon said. "We're supposed to..."

His words trailed off as he looked at them, seeing her hand in Rumiel's. His face went stiff, and his right hand tightened around his pocket watch, knuckles whitening at the pressure of his grip.

"I see," he said coldly.

He started to turn away, but Shaw gripped his arm, holding him in place.

"Ines," she said, "you don't have to say anything, but if you want to, then you can. It's okay to ask for what you want. That's part of what love's about."

The words gave Ines courage. It wasn't just their meaning. It was knowing that, no matter what, Shaw was there to help her. She could lean on someone else to see her through.

Taking a deep breath, she turned to look at Rumiel.

"You're amazing," she said to him. "You're like no one else I've ever met. So strong, so fierce, so determined. And this..." She waved a hand up and down, gesturing at his whole body. "And this..." She laid the palm of her hand against his cheek. "Just to think that you would look at me in the way you have, would think about me in the way you have, that's something that will always make me feel better about myself. I've been loved by a hero of legend, and no one can ever take that away from me.

"But I don't want to spend my life with a hero from legend. I can't feel close to that. Your whole life is so different, so distant from mine, I would never feel like we really shared our hearts. I want you as a friend and as a champion. But I love Damon. And if, after all this, he'll still have me, I want to be with him."

Rumiel nodded solemnly.

"So be it." He leaned forwards and kissed her on the forehead. "I will always be there for you, Ines Salgado, as a friend and as a champion. I too have been made better by what has passed between us, and I will be forever grateful for that."

He swept her into his arms, and they hugged each other tightly. As they separated, Ines took a deep breath and turned to look at the others. Damon looked bewildered, while Shaw was stifling a smile.

A bell tolled out a single deep note.

"It's time," Shaw said.

With her in the lead, they walked out of Bede's chapel and into the main chamber of the cathedral. The whole place was packed. Mages, soldiers, and wingless demons filled every available standing space. Angels and dark-winged creatures hovered above them, the beating of their wings the only sound.

Then chanting emerged from the far end of the cathedral, quiet at first but rising in volume. Glowing magical energy spilt out from there, pouring from Cuthbert's shrine.

Weaving their hands through the air, the mages, demons, and angels pulled down strands of that power, combining it with their own. Ines did not understand the details of what they were doing, but she could follow the big picture. Wherever a soldier stood—an ordinary man or woman without any touch of the arcane—the others passed strands of magic to them. The soldiers stared in amazement but kept their calm as they twisted the strands together. In their hands, the different magics were bound—currents of black, white, and sparkling grey turning to rainbows of dazzling color as they flowed together.

By now, Ines had progressed to the center of the cathedral. There, the rainbow strands of magic were passed to her. She could feel the power thrumming through her, and she gasped as her whole body tingled and glowed.

"No!" A bright figure came soaring in through a broken window. The archangel Michael drew his sword as he hovered above Ines's head. "This shall not pass," he said, slashing at the strands of magic around him. They split and fell, their power lost. "To me, Blazing Host! Find your strength, and set this world to right!"

The magic still flowed through Ines, but something in it was changed. It felt weaker, less focused. If this continued, then everything could be lost.

The angels flew forward, forming a circle around Michael. Ines watched with tears in her eyes. They had come so close, and now...

Rumiel rose in majesty, his glow illuminating the carved stones of the cathedral and the faces of the people gathered there.

"No more," he said sadly. "Brother Michael, you know only violence, and you bring only ruin. It is not for you to set the world to right when you have done so much wrong."

"Traitor!" Michael snarled. "Blasphemer. Seize him, my host. Let Rumiel be cast down into the darkness where he belongs."

The angels closed in, but it was not Rumiel that they laid their hands on. It was Michael.

"No!" he bellowed, struggling against them.

"Him, not me!" he screamed as Helda tore the sword from his hands.

"You will ruin everything!" he cried out as they dragged him to the ground, binding his arms, wings, and legs with glowing chains, silencing him with a gag torn from another angel's robes.

Then they returned to the spell.

In wonder, Ines felt the power surge through her once more, rich and unstoppable. Its strands came together and then separated, spreading out to become a net and then a sheet, something that was both within and above the world around her. She felt it spread out through the rest of Durham and was aware of each building and person it touched. Then she felt it sweep on, across Britain, across Europe, across the world. The whole of the Earth seemed to sit inside her soul at once. She was everything, and everything was her.

It was wonderful.

And then it was over. She opened her eyes and found herself standing in a cathedral in which hundreds of people were smiling at each other.

"You did it!" Marklew rushed up and hugged her until she felt she might disappear into his vast bulk. "You wonderful, brilliant girl, you did it!"

Other people slapped her back, shook her hand, wrapped their arms around her. There was cheering and laughter all around. Even the soldiers, who only half understood what had happened, were grinning and staring in amazement at their own hands, hands that moments before had been weaving magic.

Ines's mother came over and hugged her.

"You were right," Julie Salgado said. "I am so proud."

"Thanks, Mum," Ines said.

A strange realization came over her. She still loved her mother, and she was still pleased to have her approval, but that approval wasn't everything in the world, as it once had been. She wasn't a little girl anymore.

Together, they walked out of the cathedral along with the rest. Palace Green was filled with excited chatter. Someone had found a guitar and was starting to sing a celebratory song.

The angels gathered in the center of the green, Michael held by two of them. Rumiel waved, and Ines went over to join them. She was surprised to see that he had been talking with Damon, the two boys smiling.

"It is time for us to go," Rumiel said. "This new Barrier of Mercy will not let those of the other realms remain on

Earth except by human invitation. As it grows in strength, it will cast us out."

"We could invite you to stay," Damon said. "If you want."

Rumiel shook his head.

"We have work to do," he said. "Like you, we have to rebuild, to find a new way of being after all that has passed. Farewell, Damon Lorus." He shook Damon's hand. "Farewell, Ines Salgado." He hugged her briefly one last time. "God smile upon you all."

He rose from the ground, flying slowly at first up into the night sky. With a great beating of wings, the other angels followed him, rising towards the heavens. Their bright bodies shone against the darkness, moving faster and faster as they went, becoming distant figures and then tiny dots that merged with the stars and were gone.

Behind them, the whole crowd clapped and cheered, even Eldervain and the demons.

Ines took Damon's hand. Together, they walked away towards the edge of the crowd and some much-needed privacy.

CHAPTER 24
A Reckoning

At the edge of Palace Green, a paved footpath ran between the library and another building, running towards the steep-sloped bank above the river. A single streetlight flickered in the alleyway, its rhythm as fast and erratic as the beating of Ines's heart. She drew Damon into the alley with her, away from the gazes of their friends and comrades.

"So, um..." Damon grinned as he looked down at her, lost for words. "Now what?"

"Now this." Stretching up on tiptoes, Ines wrapped her arms around his neck and kissed him hard on the lips. For a moment, they stood like that, unmoving, then his hands were on her back, pressing her against him in the urgency of desire, fingers running up her spine. He ran a hand through her hair then down her side until it rested on her hip. The rest of the world vanished from her thoughts as she clasped him close.

At last, they separated, laughing giddily as they gasped for breath.

"That was..." Ines said then realized that nothing she said could do the moment justice.

"Wasn't it just," Damon said, grinning.

The alley widened farther down, and there was a set of stone steps leading up to an old door on one side. Arms around each other, they went to sit on the step. There were more kisses, her hands running over his arms, his chest, his face, enjoying every inch of him.

Behind them, the sounds of celebration grew. Guitars and drums, singing and chanting, laughter and cheering. The noise rose as people emerged from their hiding places around the city and came to see what was happening. It became a joyful tumult unlike anything heard for months in Durham, perhaps in the whole of England.

"Just to be clear," Damon said during a pause, "does this mean that we're... I mean to say that will we be—"

"This is you being clear?" Ines asked, laughing.

"I don't think I'm the one who needs to be clearer about this stuff," Damon said, his eyes showing a little of the hurt that had come from hearing about her and Rumiel.

"That's fair," she said. "And I'm sorry. And yes, if you'll have me, then this means that we are..."

She felt awkward saying it, so instead, she kissed him.

The streetlamp gave a final loud buzz and then went out.

"Looks like the city wanted us to have some privacy," Ines said, running her fingers along the back of Damon's neck.

Not everyone was in on the city's plans. Footsteps approached from the darkened end of the path, down towards the river. The clack of a single pair of feet on dirt and stone announcing another arrival for the party. Feeling awkward at the thought of someone watching their private moment, Ines disentangled herself from Damon, and he did the same. They sat at opposite sides of the stairs, cold air between them, only the tips of their fingers touching as they rested on the step, a thrilling reminder of what they had been doing and what was to come.

In the darkness of the alley, the footsteps stopped. A figure was just visible, a blacker shape against a world of deep nighttime grey.

"Party's up there," Damon said cheerfully, the wave of his arm just visible in the darkness.

"I'm not here to celebrate," the figure replied in a voice as cold as ice.

A magical claw appeared before them. The glow of its power illuminated the pinstripe suit and fiercely regal face of Elizabeth Oldfield.

"Hey!" Ines yelled as she leapt to her feet. Her shout was lost amid the rowdy noises filling the night. "Help!"

"No one can help you now," Oldfield growled.

A scraping sound made Ines look up. A stone lion perched on the edge of the roof, ready to pounce. She pushed Damon one way and flung herself the other as the creature leapt, crashing onto the steps between them. Chunks of stone and iron railings flew through the air, battering Ines and clattering against the walls.

The creature turned to face her, baring its grey teeth. One foreleg was cracked where it had hit the ground, but it was still a menacing sight.

The lion lunged at Ines. She rolled forward, beneath the arc of its attack, and sprang to her feet behind it, grabbing one of the broken railings as she went. Twisting around, she was just in time to duck the sweep of a stone paw.

The lion advanced, pressing her back against the wall. As it raised its good paw again, Ines grasped the railing in both hands and swung it as hard as she could at the cracked leg. Her shoulder jolted with pain at the impact, but there was a crash, and the leg flew apart.

Its balance destroyed, the lion toppled forwards, face smashing into the stones. Raising her improvised weapon, Ines beat it again and again against the back of that stone head, until every muscle in her arms ached and the magical beast lay still, its face reduced to gravel.

Flushed and angry, she turned to face Oldfield. As she did, her blood ran cold.

Damon stood in the middle of the alley. Chains of pure magical energy were wrapped around him, binding his arms to his sides. Blood ran from a claw wound across his face. Oldfield stood behind him, her claws up against his throat, the shattered remains of his pocket watch gleaming beneath her heel.

"You think you've won, but you haven't," Oldfield said. "I ripped the Barrier open before. I can do it again. That power will be mine to use. To shape the world to something better than what we have. A place where angels and demons have no part. A place for humans. Only humans. A place ruled by the wise and the strong."

"Please," Ines said, "let him go. This can't help you."

"Oh, but it can," Oldfield replied. "I know how much he means to you, and how much you mean to our new minister. And then there's his father—what might Chron do for the sake of his heir?"

Damon laughed bitterly then stopped as the claws pressed against his flesh.

"Come, demon-spawn," Oldfield said. "We have a world to transform."

She backed off down the alley, taking Damon with her. At the end, she turned to the left and, pushing him ahead of her, disappeared from view.

Rage sang in Ines's mind. A symphony of death and destruction, of all the terrible things that Oldfield had done and the terrible things that should happen to her. The sounds of her allies celebrating still reached Ines from the green, but she ignored them.

This was for her to deal with.

Keeping hold of the iron bar from the railings, she crept down the alley. At the end, only moonlight illuminated the path leading off to her left, between thin lines of trees and shrubs. She followed it, the ground uneven beneath her feet, the iron heavy in her hand.

The path sloped down. Ahead, she could see the glow of light from Oldfield's claw and the magic binding Damon. It was too faint to add more than the slightest illumination to the steep slope on the left and the flat riverbank to the right.

Oldfield hesitated at the riverbank. Ines kept creeping down the path towards her. Fragments of muted conversation drifted through the night.

"What do you mean, you don't know?" Oldfield hissed. "You people have been here for weeks, plotting and scheming the ruin of the world."

"We didn't spend much time boating," Damon said. "Or looking at bridges. I know two ways across, and they're both back where we came from."

"I see through your trick," Oldfield said. "You want to take me back so she can rescue you."

"I wouldn't take you anywhere near Ines," Damon said. "I love her. Why would I put her in danger?"

"Love her?" Oldfield said. "What do you know about love at your age? I knew love. A child of my own, part of me and yet apart, our lives wrapped around each other. That's what those monsters took away from me. That's what—"

A twig snapped beneath Ines's foot as she reached the riverbank. Oldfield whirled around, the magical light casting her face into patches of bright illumination and deep shadow. She squinted into the darkness, not seeing Ines.

"Who's there?" Oldfield hissed. "Is that you, Salgado brat?"

Slowly and silently, Ines circled closer. Oldfield narrowed her eyes, trying to peer through light so close that all it did was ruin her night vision.

"I'll kill him," Oldfield said, placing the claws again next to Damon's neck.

"No," Damon said. "Ines, do it."

He jerked suddenly forwards. The claws caught the side of his neck as he lurched away from Oldfield and flung himself to the ground.

Ines leapt. She swung the bar straight into the side of Oldfield's face. Blood and teeth flew, and the mage staggered back.

As Ines strode forward, Oldfield raised her claw. But her arm was wobbling and her eyes wide with shock. Another blow from Ines caught her on the elbow, and she screamed, her arm going limp.

With blow after blow, Ines pressed Oldfield back, knocking her to her knees and then to the ground. The woman curled up, arms wrapped around her face, as Ines poured all her fury into her, hitting her again and again and again and-

"Ines!" Damon croaked. "Don't do it!"

She looked over to see him lying on the ground. His bonds had dissipated, their light gone, but even in the moonlight, she could see that his skin was pale, blood running through his hands as he clutched at his neck.

Fury rose all the stronger in her. Oldfield had almost killed her boyfriend and best friend.

She raised the bar and stood over Oldfield, ready to finish her off.

Oldfield was crying. Her hands were clasped in front of her face, not sheltering it from the impending attack but holding a locket for her to look at in her final moments. Ines couldn't see the photo, but she realized with horrible clarity who must be shown there.

"I'm so sorry, baby," Oldfield whispered. "I almost found a way to make you better, to keep you safe, but I failed. I'm so sorry."

Her voice wavered as she stared at the picture of her daughter, locked in a coma for all these years. The thing that

had twisted her up inside, turning her towards anger, hate, and a lust for power.

Just as her actions had twisted up Ines.

The metal bar hit the ground with a thud.

"I'm here," Ines said, crouching beside Damon. She tore a strip off her hoodie and wrapped it around his neck, an improvised bandage over the claw wound. "I'll help you get back to help."

"What about her?" Damon asked.

"She's not going anywhere," Ines said, glancing at the battered and pitiful figure of the former minister. "We can send someone down to take her into custody."

"And then?"

"And then I don't know," she said, helping him to his feet. "A lot of people have done terrible things, things that they wouldn't have normally. Things driven by dark emotions, by overexcitement, by angels or demons or orders from above. Some people might need to be punished, to show that the rules still stand. But some might need to be forgiven too. I don't think it's up to us to choose which are which."

"You're probably right," Damon said, leaning on her as they headed back up the path. "After all, we're among the guilty parties. We brought down a government department."

"And fought against British soldiers," Ines added. "That's probably treason."

"Broke into a pub—that's burglary and trespassing."

"Stole a train."

"Not just a train—food, clothes, other things we needed."

"Then there's all the vandalism."

"And we've been playing truant from school for weeks now."

"We're bad people."

"The worst." Damon squeezed her shoulder. "I love you, Ines Salgado."

"I love you too. But don't you have to go rule a demonic host now?"

Damon took a deep breath. "Yeah, about that..."

CHAPTER 25
A Whole New World

Ines rolled over in bed and rubbed the sleep from her eyes. Through the blur of early morning, she tried to make out the numbers on her alarm clock. She remembered it going off, then she'd rolled over to rest for five more minutes, and now—

"Oh no!" She bolted upright. It was over an hour since the alarm had gone off. She was going to be late for school.

She leapt out of bed and hunted hurriedly for clothes. A crumpled pair of jeans lying near the door. A clean T-shirt hanging over her chair. The new mouse hoodie that Marklew had given her as a going-away present when she left Durham.

Having snatched up her backpack and trainers, she rushed out of the door and raced down the stairs.

"I'm up!" she said as she ran into the kitchen. "Is there any breakfast?"

"I saved you eggs on toast," Dad said, smiling at her from beside the stove.

"No fair!" Toby exclaimed. "You said I couldn't have any if I got up late. Ines is late. Why does she get them?"

"Because Ines didn't need to get a magic lesson in before school," Mum said, smiling across her cup of coffee. "Don't you want to be a great mage like us?"

"No," Toby said. "I want to be a racing car driver." A thoughtful expression crossed his face. "Or maybe a hero, like Ines, but not as annoying."

"Toby," Mum said, "you apologize to your sister."

"Sorry you're so annoying," Toby said.

"Toby Salgado!"

"It's okay," Ines said, tousling her brother's hair until he squirmed in his seat. "Not everyone can be as great as me."

"I hope you're not like this at school," Dad said, putting a plate in front of her.

"No one at school knows what I did," Ines said. "Not much chance to show off."

As she set to devouring scrambled eggs on toast, she glanced over at the TV in the corner of the kitchen. A familiar face was on screen, behind a row of microphones.

"Look," she said through a mouthful of food. "Tamsin."

Dad turned up the volume. Though Tamsin Shaw was visible talking on screen, the voice they heard was that of a newscaster explaining events.

"...unprecedented news conference late yesterday at which Tamsin Shaw, Minister for Occult Affairs, spoke about her impending appearance before the Select Committee on the Civil War."

"There is much to be explained," Shaw said. She looked as calm and professional as anyone Ines had ever seen on the news, the scars on her cheek only adding to the seriousness of her presence. "Things that have been unjustly withheld from the public by previous holders of this post. It is my hope that my appearance before the committee can help in healing the scars not just of our recent conflict but of generations of wrongs committed in the name of public safety."

"The existence of the Ministry remains controversial months after it was revealed to the public," the newscaster said. "Shaw herself, suddenly cast into the spotlight, has become a figure of personal as well as political scandal, with rumors of an affair between her and her deputy, Hema—"

Dad muted the TV.

"Affair indeed." He shook his head. "It wouldn't even be worth mentioning if she weren't a minister. Those two are so close, they might as well be married."

Ines avoided catching anyone's eye and focused on her eggs. Unlike the rest of her family, she had attended a small civil wedding in the Ministry building a few weeks before. She even had a bridesmaid dress hidden in her wardrobe, a memento of that happy but very secretive day. Shaw might be a public figure, but she liked to keep her personal life private.

"I'm all done," Ines said, pushing away her plate. "Thanks, Dad. I should get going."

As she picked up her bag, she paused to savor the moment. After all the months of struggle and turmoil, it was wonderful to be back home, the house in order, with her family around her. That was something she would never tire of. Coming so close to losing it made it all the more precious.

"Is your boyfriend coming to pick you up?" Toby said in a mocking singsong tone.

"No, brother dearest," Ines said, making him squirm again as she wrapped him in a hug. "I'm meeting him on the way to school."

She let go of Toby and stepped over to kiss Dad on the cheek. "Thanks for breakfast."

She hugged Mum, slipped on her trainers, and headed out the door.

The street was quiet. Most of this part of Barnett was quiet in the mornings. Not everyone had come home after the troubles. Those who remained hadn't all started back at school or work yet. Rebuilding wasn't just about replacing houses and offices lost to war and riots.

It was about rebuilding the social structures of daily life, and that wasn't easy.

As she walked down the road, Ines saw signs of the good work that had been done so far. The houses on their street had all been repaired, apart from one so badly damaged that it had been bulldozed and replaced with a park. The shop on the corner had a sign up saying that it would reopen next week. There wasn't even much noise of heavy machinery, construction work having moved on to the next neighborhood. Slowly but surely, the world was being rebuilt.

She stopped at the corner and closed her eyes. Spreading out her fingers, she felt the faintest tingling in her skin. A sense of pressing against something that wasn't quite there. Something that was in the air around her and yet not in the world at all.

The Barrier of Mercy. Her Barrier of Mercy. Something born through her efforts and those of so many people precious to her. A spell to protect and empower the whole world. A magic that made it easier to heal and to rebuild, as well as to hold powerful forces at bay. Ever since that magic ran through her in Durham Cathedral, she had been able to feel its presence. There was a connection that would never entirely go away, and she wondered what it meant for her future. Was this her magic now, or something else, something that recognised just how un-magical she was?

"Lovely day, isn't it?" Damon said. "Perfect for sitting in a darkened, airless classroom learning about atomic bonds."

As Ines opened her eyes, she saw him standing in front of her, dressed in his usual black shirt and trousers, with a long coat over it to keep out the cold. He gave her a lopsided smile.

"Hello to you too," she said, leaning forward to kiss him. Then she turned to smile at the figure beside him. "And good morning to you, Eldervain."

"Good?" Eldervain had the brim of his hat pulled down at the front to hide the sagging, inhuman aspect of his face. "You creatures have no idea of what is good. I have seen fire rain from the skies and acid boil from the ground. I have seen the living fall in bloody heaps upon the shattered earth and the dead rise to devour all around them. I have seen blizzards of razorblades upon a plateau of ancient skin. And you try to tell me that a blue sky is good."

"You don't have to stay up here," Damon said. "Someone else could carry the orders for my host down to Hell."

"No one else will take this most wretched of posts," Eldervain said, shaking his head. "Even though I tell them "soon he will be done with his learning and come to command us.""

"Maybe," Damon said. "Though I'm thinking of going to uni, might even do a PhD. You could be stuck up here for a while."

"There are worse things," Eldervain conceded. "After fighting to save this place, I feel... not fond, but invested in its fate."

"Lovely," Ines said. "Now why don't you go invest in some other part of it while Damon and I go to school?"

"As you command, Mistress of the Host." Eldervain made a mocking bow and then vanished into the shadows between buildings.

"Let's go learn," Ines said.

"In a few minutes," Damon said. "I've got a surprise for you first."

Taking her hand—something else she would never tire of—he led her down the street, around the corner, and across the front of a pub with a Reopening Soon sign outside. Walking down the drive at its side, they emerged into a car park out back.

"If this is your idea of romance, then you might be getting dumped," Ines said.

"Not romance," Damon said. "Something else. Something I thought you might want a little privacy for."

She looked around. Aside from the pub itself, the car park was surrounded on two sides by wooden fences and on the third by a tall hedgerow. Those bushes rustled, and a white-clad figure pushed out between them.

"Rumiel!" She ran over and hugged him. "What are you doing here? I thought that you couldn't come back into our world."

"Not without invitation," he said, smiling at Damon. "But I wanted to see you once more, to celebrate your return to school, to your family, to the life that was torn from you on the day we met."

She hugged him harder.

"Not everything about that day was bad," she said. Then she took a step back. "Would you like to come and hang out with us this evening? No one's going to expect us to do homework on the first school day after the apocalypse."

Rumiel shook his head.

"I am most occupied," he said, smiling. "Blessed with rank and duties I would never have dreamed to earn before. Not just angel now, but archangel, a commander of the hosts, a leader of my kind."

"I'm so proud," she said.

"I could not be what I am without you," Rumiel said. "I lost my way, but you returned me to a righteous path. And none in all the host have taught me so much about what it means to lead, to struggle, and to love. One day, we shall meet again, Ines Salgado. Until then, I hold you in my heart always."

He spread his wings wide behind him. They glowed with a golden warmth.

"Thank you, Damon," he said. "Thank you both."

Then he soared into the air and vanished in the distance.

Ines turned to Damon.

"You're amazing," she said. "After everything that happened, to bring him here for me."

Damon shrugged.

"You almost dumped me for an angel," he said. "I lead a circle of Hell. We all have things we'd be better off without, but everything I can do to make you happy, I will."

"Then come here," Ines said.

He did, and she kissed him. It made her very happy.

ABOUT THE AUTHOR

S.A. Beck lives in sunny California. When she's not surfing, knitting or daydreaming in a hammock, she's writing novels.

www.ingramcontent.com/pod-product-compliance
Lightning Source LLC
Chambersburg PA
CBHW032149190626
46814CB00005BA/1901